THE HAUNTED TOWER

Susannah Leigh

Illustrated by Brenda Haw

Designed by
Brian Robertson and Kim Blundell

Edited by Karen Dolby

Additional puzzles by Sarah Dixon and Roy Preston

Series Editor: Gaby Waters

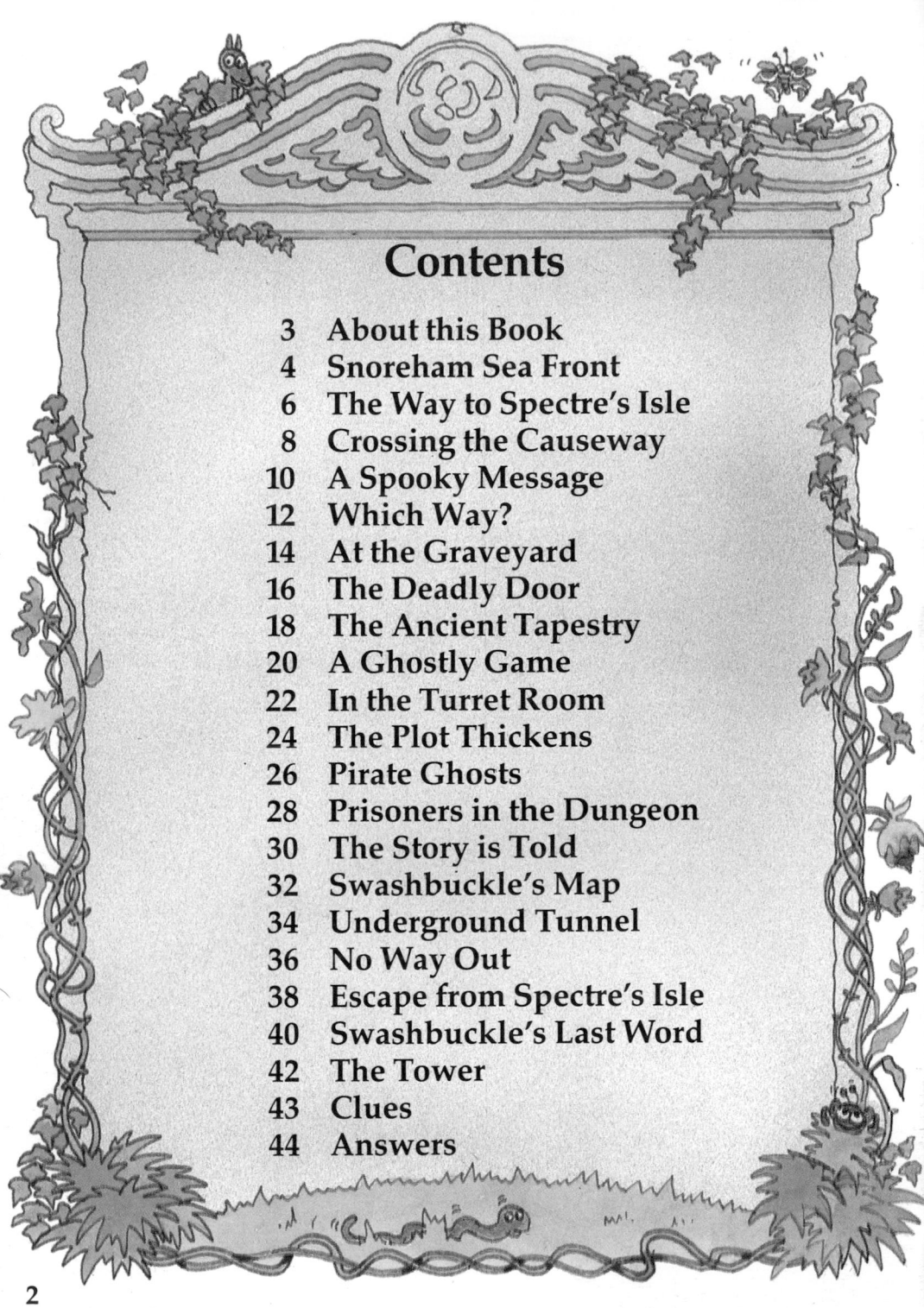

Contents

About this Book

The Haunted Tower is a spooky adventure story with a difference. The difference is that you can take part in the adventure.

Throughout the book, there are lots of ghostly puzzles and perplexing problems which you must solve in order to understand the next part of the story.

Look at the pictures carefully and watch out for vital clues. Sometimes you will need to flick back through the book to help you find an answer. There are extra clues on page 43 and you can check the answers on pages 44 to 48.

Just turn the page to begin the adventure...

Charlie

Ali

Nic

Nic and Ali are visiting their cousin Charlie at the seaside town of Port Snoreham for the first time.

Snoreham Sea Front

Charlie, Nic and Ali were busy slurping ice creams on the first afternoon of their holiday in Port Snoreham. Ali pointed at a dark, wooded island on which stood a tall, mysterious tower. She wondered what it was called.

"That's Spectre's Isle," said Charlie. "They say the tower's haunted by a ghostly pirate called Captain Swashbuckle. He built the tower hundreds of years ago and there he planned his daring sea voyages.

Then, one stormy night, his ship hit a reef off the island and sank without trace. The legend says an incredible hoard of treasure was lost with Swashbuckle and his crew, but it has never been found. Now Swashbuckle's ghost is said to haunt the tower."

Nic peered through the beach telescope for a closer look and gasped in amazement, scarcely believing her eyes. Could the legend be true?

5

The Way to Spectre's Isle

Was the tower haunted? Nic and Ali could hardly wait to investigate. But first they had to find a way to Spectre's Isle.

"No one ever dares go there," Charlie said, nervously. "Besides, it's impossible."

Ali asked some locals and was told there was a causeway across to the island, but it was usually flooded. The rest of the information was very puzzling.

But when Charlie checked the tides and Nic looked at her diary, they realized they could reach the island at a certain time of the day.

When can they cross the causeway?

Crossing the Causeway

That night, just as the numbers on Charlie's extra-tough-all-weather-underwater-survival watch changed to 00.00 hours, they arrived at the causeway.

"We're almost there," said Nic, pointing at the tower, ahead.

"Hang on," Charlie shivered. "I don't like the look of those spiky rocks or the quicksand."

Ali agreed, "And watch out for the crabs and octopusses."

"And those starfish look dangerous," gulped Charlie. "I wonder if the jellyfish are poisonous?"

"Follow me," said Nic, sounding braver than she felt.

Can you find a safe route across the causeway? Be careful!

A Spooky Message

Damp and bedraggled, they stepped ashore into a dark forest. Tall trees closed in on all sides and moonlight shone through the branches, making sinister patterns on the ground.

Through the trees, they could just see the top of the tower, shadowy and mysterious in the darkness. Slowly, they crept towards it. Charlie heard a strange, ghostly echo. Ali had a feeling they were being watched. It was very spooky.

At last they saw the tower in front of them. At the same time, two shimmering forms appeared floating in midair.

"Ghosts!" gasped Charlie, terrified by their staring white faces and glinting cutlasses.

While the trio stared in horror, the ghostly apparitions glided slowly away around the side of the tower. As they went, a small piece of paper fluttered to the ground. Feeling a bit shaky, Nic picked it up and stared at the meaningless list of words.

"What is it?" puzzled Ali, peering at the note.

"Perhaps it's a ghostly code," exclaimed Charlie, trying to work out what it meant.

What does the strange note say?

> 4.30 FRIDAY. KK FROM FF TO BB. AND TO GO GRAVEYARD THE FOR TONIGHT INFORMATION FURTHER YOU ABOUT WHO. KNOW MEET THEN IN ME TOWER THE THE AT HOUR. WITCHING TAKE YOU FLOATING THE AND PHANTOM, TO REMEMBER IT HIDE YOU WHEN THERE. GET GHOULS PS GHOSTS AND AND AWAKE THE LET BEGIN. HAUNTING MAY WE GUESTS HAVE TONIGHT.

Which Way?

Phantoms, ghouls, ghosts . . . what did it mean? And what about "you know who"? Nic was determined to find the answers and that meant going to the graveyard.

"I don't like the idea of seeing those ghosts again," Charlie gulped.

"Besides," Ali pointed out. "We don't know the way. These woods are so dark we could be wandering for ever."

But Nic had made up her mind and marched along the only path leading from the tower. Ali and Charlie had to run to keep up. Soon they came to a clearing with mysterious, overgrown paths branching off in all directions. An old, rotten signpost lay on the ground.

Looking closely at the bits, Nic thought for a moment. With a flash of inspiration, she realized they could still use the sign to find the path to the graveyard.

Which path leads to the graveyard?

At the Graveyard

At the end of the path, a chilling mist began swirling around them. Through it, they could see the tall iron gates of the graveyard and the ancient stones beyond. The shadows of the tombs lengthened eerily in the torch beam and even Nic wondered if they should go in.

Charlie hung nervously behind, while Ali and Nic ventured inside the gates. Immediately Ali spotted something odd. Lying on the ground was a large sheet of paper.

"How strange," said Ali, puzzled. "It's got holes cut in it."

RIP
170

RIP
PIRATE MERVIN

1690-1740

JACK DANIELS RESTS HERE
A PIRATE OF NOTE
DRANK A BARREL OF RUM
WHICH STUCK IN HIS THROAT
~ RIP ~

HERE LIES
FERDINAND FILLET
1704 ~ 1735
1ST MATE OF THE
'SKULL & CROSS BONES'
WHO MET HIS UNTIMELY
DEATH ON THIS ISLE
AT THE WRONG END
OF SWASHBUCKLE'S
SWORD

HERE LIE THE BONES OF
DAVY JONES
A PIRATE OF NOBLE BIRTH
HE FEASTED ON PIGS
AND MOUNTAINS OF FIGS
WHICH EXPLAIN HIS
EXTRAORDINARY GIRTH

19TH JULY 1736

REST IN PEACE
PRETTY POLL
TRUSTY COMPANION
AND LOYAL FRIEND TO
SEPTIMUS SWASHBUCKLE
THERE NEVER LIVED
A GREATER PARROT

21ST JUNE 1726

HIS FINAL HOUR
WAS SPENT IN THE TOWER
AS A PRISONER BOUND IN CHAINS
POOR WILLIAM SLAUGHTER
DIED SOONER THAN HE OUGHTER
AND LOST ALL HIS
ILL GOTTEN GAINS

ALBERT LIES HERE
A BRAVE BUCCANEER
ASHE LAY IN HIS BED
SOMEONE CUT OFF HIS HEAD

1706-1736

Nic looked at the paper and realized it was exactly the same size as some of the gravestones. This gave her an idea. She was sure she was right.

"This paper is more valuable than you think," she exclaimed. "It's the key to a message."

Can you read the message?

The Deadly Door

They looked at each other in horror. Who could the prisoner be and why was he doomed to die? Could they save him, or were they already too late? The only way to find out was to return to the tower.

They raced back through the woods and tiptoed around the tower looking for a way in.

"Over here," Ali hissed to the other two. "We can get in this way."

Charlie wasn't too pleased at this. He would have liked an excuse to turn around and leave. Even Nic's teeth were chattering as they tiptoed up the steps and under the portcullis. Would they see the ghosts again?

Inside the coast was clear, but getting into the rest of the tower was not going to be so easy. Facing them was a solid wooden door, bolted and barred by a heavy beam. They tried hard, but could not move it.

It was then they noticed a lever attached to a cog mechanism. It seemed to be an elaborate lock and the only way of opening the door. Charlie ran up the short flight of stone steps and grasped the lever.

"Watch out!" called Ali. "If you turn the handle the wrong way that enormous spiky cannon ball will fall on you!"

Which way must Charlie turn the handle?

The Ancient Tapestry

Inside the door was a winding stone staircase. Slowly the trio made their way up. At the top an old door creaked as Nic pushed against it. The three peered in to see suits of armour, glinting in the darkness.

They crept into the dimly-lit room. It looked as if no one had been in there for years. Then Charlie spotted an old piece of cloth tucked between a suit of armour and the wall. It looked interesting.

BAND OF BUCCANEERS AND BUILDER OF THE

HIS TOWER TO DIE AND HERE HE PLANS TO HIDE

hand sewn by Mrs Noggins, loyal tower-keeper

CAT, COMMANDER OF A BRAVE

WOUNDED IN BATTLE HE RETURNS TO

GREEDY HANDS x x x x x x

AMASSES A HOARD OF

He tugged hard. With a great RIP the material came away from its hiding place. At that moment, there was a loud rumbling sound and the whole ceiling began to give way. They dashed out of the room just in time.

Charlie looked at the material as it fell to pieces. It was a tapestry. The pictures were torn and muddled, but bit by bit he was able to read the story.

What does the tapestry say?

TOWER LEADS A LIFE OF ADVENTURE ON THE HIGH SEAS AND

HIS PRECIOUS HOARD FROM PRYING EYES AND

to Captain Swashbuckle, in April 1741.

TREASURE AND PRICELESS JEWELS, MORTALLY

SEPTIMUS SWASHBUCKLE, CAPTAIN OF THE PEPPERY

A Ghostly Game

So the old legend was wrong. Swashbuckle's treasure wasn't at the bottom of the sea after all. It seemed to be hidden somewhere in the tower. But where was it? In front of them, in the dust-filled corridor, was an open door. Were there more clues inside?

Quickly they slipped into the room. The door clicked tightly shut behind them. A strange, yellow light flickered all around and in the shadows they could see furniture, a small spiral staircase and...

"Ghosts!" gasped Charlie.

I'll search the armour room and have a look downstairs. You two go upstairs and scour the turret and battlements.

No, Brian. You look in here. Katy and I will search the rest of this floor and check downstairs.

Codswallop, Fred. We'll look around here. Brian can search the turret and battlements.

Three shadowy figures sat huddled around a large table in the middle of the room. They were surrounded by bottles and candles and were whispering fiercely to one another.

The door had locked. There was no choice but to hide and hope the ghosts didn't notice them. Hardly daring to breathe and with knees knocking, they listened to the spooky voices.

After what seemed like hours, the ghoulish conversation ended. The ghostly figures slowly stood up, about to begin their mysterious search. Nic breathed a sigh of relief. She knew what to do now.

"Don't panic," she whispered. "I know where we can go to get away from those ghouls."

Which pirate has the highest score?
Which part of the tower is safe?

In the Turret Room

Lend us a fiver.

Before the ghosts turned round, Nic, Charlie and Ali dashed up the spiral stairs to the turret room. It looked as if it had not been disturbed for centuries. As their eyes got used to the dark, they realized this wasn't true. Then Ali spotted something which proved someone else had been in the room VERY recently.

What has Ali spotted?
What other odd things are there?

23

The Plot Thickens

HISTORIAN VANISHES

by Will E. Tell

Lord R. Kive

POLICE ARE INVESTI-GATING the mysterious disappearance of Lord Reggie Kive from his Port Snoreham home on Monday evening. Lord Kive is a well known historian and expert on Snoreham.

Kive made his most exciting discovery only weeks ago when he uncovered the long lost wreck of "The Peppery Cat", a 17th century pirate ship. It was owned by the notorious Captain Septimus Swashbuckle whose ghost is supposed to haunt the tower on Spectre's Isle.

Swashbuckle's Hoard

Legend tells of Swashbuckle's fantastic hoard of priceless treasure. It was thought the hoard sank with Swashbuckle and his ship, but when Kive's team of divers recovered the wreck, no treasure was found.

No Clues

Rumour has it that Kive was on the point of discovering the secret of Swashbuckle's treasure when he vanished without trace. Police are treating his disappearance as suspicious, but as yet have no firm leads.

Mystery

Lord Kive's housekeeper, Mrs Kleenupp, said when interviewed yesterday, "Larks-a-mercy dearies, it's not like him to go off without saying anything. He always leaves a note. Something terrible must have happened . . ."

HORROR SCOPE

Predicted for you by Ann Dromeda.

AQUARIUS
The full moon could bring some changes to your life.

PISCES
Beware of new events. Something fishy is going on.

ARIES
It's a good time to move house. You have been feeling restless.

TAURUS
Take the bull by the horns and explore undiscovered territory.

GEMINI
Your fear of the unknown will grow greater this month.

CANCER
Don't let unexplained events put you off exploring new horizons.

LEO
You will meet a tall, dark, shadowy figure.

VIRGO
People from the past may well be on your mind.

LIBRA
Lately, you have been feeling like a different person.

SCORPIO
You will soon be making a journey across water.

SAGITTARIUS
A well-kept secret will be revealed to you.

CAPRICORN
Even your best laid plans will go astray.

WEATHER FORECAST
Coastal areas will experience sunshine and warmer weather, but offshore islands will suffer thunder storms and occasional lightning flashes.

Charlie reached up and grabbed the newspaper. It fell open at the middle pages and a familiar name caught his eye.

Swashbuckle! He began reading the story when suddenly he noticed something interesting about the crossword.

CROSSWORD CLUES

ACROSS

1 Season between Spring and Autumn.
3 Scurrying creatures. Like mice, but larger.
(5) Relates to the time before noon and p.m.
(7) Caught without means of escape.
10 "For _____ and _____. Amen." What word is missing?
12 Close fitting short coat of soldier or policeman.
(13) Myself.
(15) Word that is used for a male.
(17) "The Wind _____ _____ Willows." What words are missing? (2 letters. 3 letters.)
18 Sound of a bell.
(21) Underground cell. Place for a fantasy game with a dragon!
22 Mum and Dad are sometimes called Ma and _____?
24 Not at all fast.
(25) Polite word to use when asking for something.

DOWN

1 Large area of salt water.
2 A rebellion where men refuse to obey officers.
3 Stout cord that might be used as a lasso.
4 Rise and fall of the sea.
6 Good friend.
(8) Place in which information or records are stored.
9 Adam's partner in the Garden of Eden.
11 Small kind of deer.
13 What kind of maid is half-woman and half-fish?
(14) Right away. Immediately. (2 letters. 4 letters)
(15) Assist. Lend a hand.
16 Kind of antelope.
19 Sacred image or statue.
20 Wear away by biting.
23 She drank her cocoa and _____ her supper.

Some of the clues had been ringed with black ink. It seemed very odd. Quickly he set about solving them.

At last things began to click into place.

What has Charlie worked out?

Pirate Ghosts

The vanishing historian, Lord R. Kive was the prisoner in the tower! His plea for help sounded desperate. There was still a chance they could save him if they moved fast. Charlie led the way to the dungeon. But halfway down, Nic realized they were not alone. A large, mean-looking pirate was hot on their trail.

Charlie hurtled towards the bottom step. Before he could stop himself, he crashed BANG into a surprisingly solid pirate ghost, standing at the foot of the stairs. At that moment, another ghastly spectre appeared. Nic, Charlie and Ali were surrounded with no hope of escape.

There was silence for one terrible minute. Ali looked at the pirates more closely. She realized these "ghosts" were very human. In fact, she even knew their names.

"You made a big mistake meddling with us," sneered one of the pirates, picking himself up. "Now we have no choice but to imprison you here . . . for ever."

"Yes," sniggered the woman, marching them off. "It's down to the dungeon with you three."

Who are the pirate "ghosts"?

Home Sweet Home

Prisoners in the Dungeon

BANG. The door was slammed shut and locked firmly behind them. Charlie heard Fred Fillet's evil cackles floating down the corridor.

"Hah, hah, hah. I hope you enjoy your final anchoring place, me hearties," he chortled.

Was this the end for them all? Were they to be left for ever in the dark and dreary dungeon, doomed to die?

Suddenly, from out of the shadows shuffled a small, dishevelled-looking figure. He stepped into the light and they gasped in amazement. He could only be…

"Lord Kive," exclaimed Charlie.

"Pleased to meet you," said Kive. "So I WAS right. I knew there was someone else in the tower."

He explained that the foul fiends, Bream, Fillet and Krayfish had kidnapped him and brought him to the tower. He hid his plea for help in the crossword and managed to leave the newspaper in the turret room when he was taken there for interrogation.

"But why did they kidnap you?" asked Ali.

"I'll explain later, m'dear," he said. "First, we must escape."

There was a small, open window, but it was impossible to reach even standing on each others' shoulders. Ali sat down miserably on the damp, sandy floor and without thinking, built a castle.

"How can you play silly games at a time like this?" Nic started to say, when a brilliant escape plan began to form in her head.

What is Nic's escape plan?

The Story is Told

Nic and Ali helped Lord Kive to his feet after he had scrambled through the bushes.

"Phew, that was a hefty climb," he wheezed.

"But I think you'll agree it was a clever idea, sir," Nic boasted.

"Indeed it was m'dear. But there's no time to lose. Those crooks will soon realize we've gone and then there'll be trouble."

Ali was still puzzled. She wanted to know what was going on. What were Fillet and his fishy crew up to? And why had Kive been held prisoner in the tower? As they brushed themselves down, Kive began to tell them his story.

After months searching, I discovered where the wreck of Swashbuckle's ship was lying. I was sure the treasure did exist and sent down divers to explore.

No booty was found, but the diving team returned with a sealed casket, filled with Swashbuckle's papers. Among them was a map of Spectre's Isle.

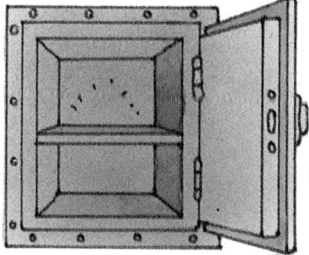

The map belonged to Swashbuckle and it seemed to pinpoint the whereabouts of his treasure.

That night, there was a burglary at my house. Fillet and his two cronies stole the old map.

But the clues on it are fiendishly difficult and the thieves couldn't work them out.

Knowing my reputation for code breaking, the villains returned. They blindfolded and kidnapped me and brought me, a prisoner, to the tower.

They threatened me and tried to force me to help them in their ruthless quest for the treasure. But I have managed to resist their demands.

Swashbuckle's Map

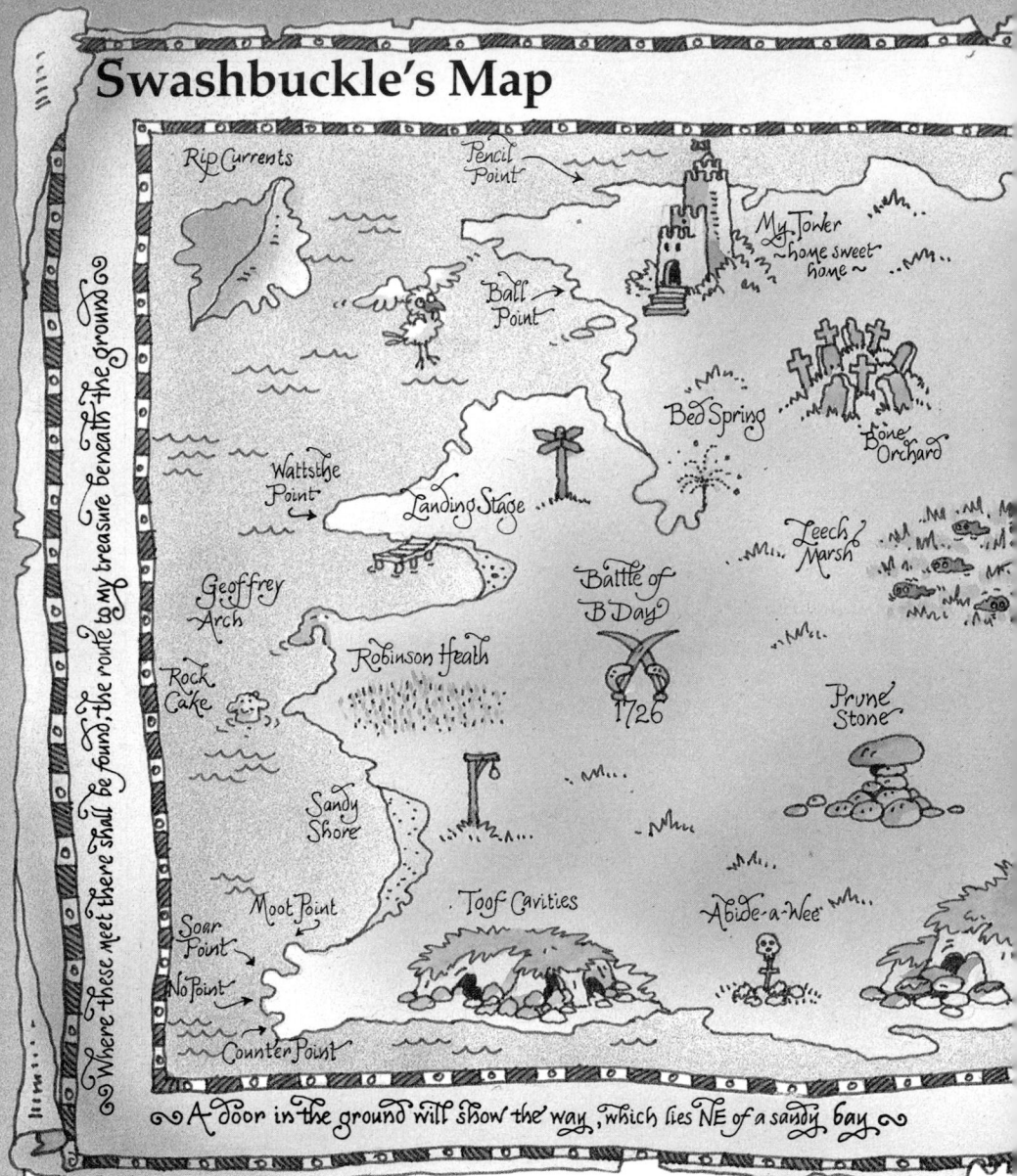

Rip Currents

Pencil Point

My Tower
~home sweet home~

Ball Point

Bed Spring

Bone Orchard

Wattsthe Point

Landing Stage

Leech Marsh

Geoffrey Arch

Battle of B Day

1726

Prune Stone

Rock Cake

Robinson Heath

Sandy Shore

Moot Point

Toof Cavities

Abide-a-Wee

Soar Point

No Point

Counter Point

Where these meet there shall be found, the route to my treasure beneath the ground

A door in the ground will show the way, which lies NE of a sandy bay

A ll of a sudden Charlie remembered the tapestry he had found.

"It seems to say the treasure's hidden in the tower," he said.

"Then my map should lead us to it," Lord Kive said, excitedly. "I have it safe here in my pocket. Those vile villains gave it back to me so that I could decipher the clues for them."

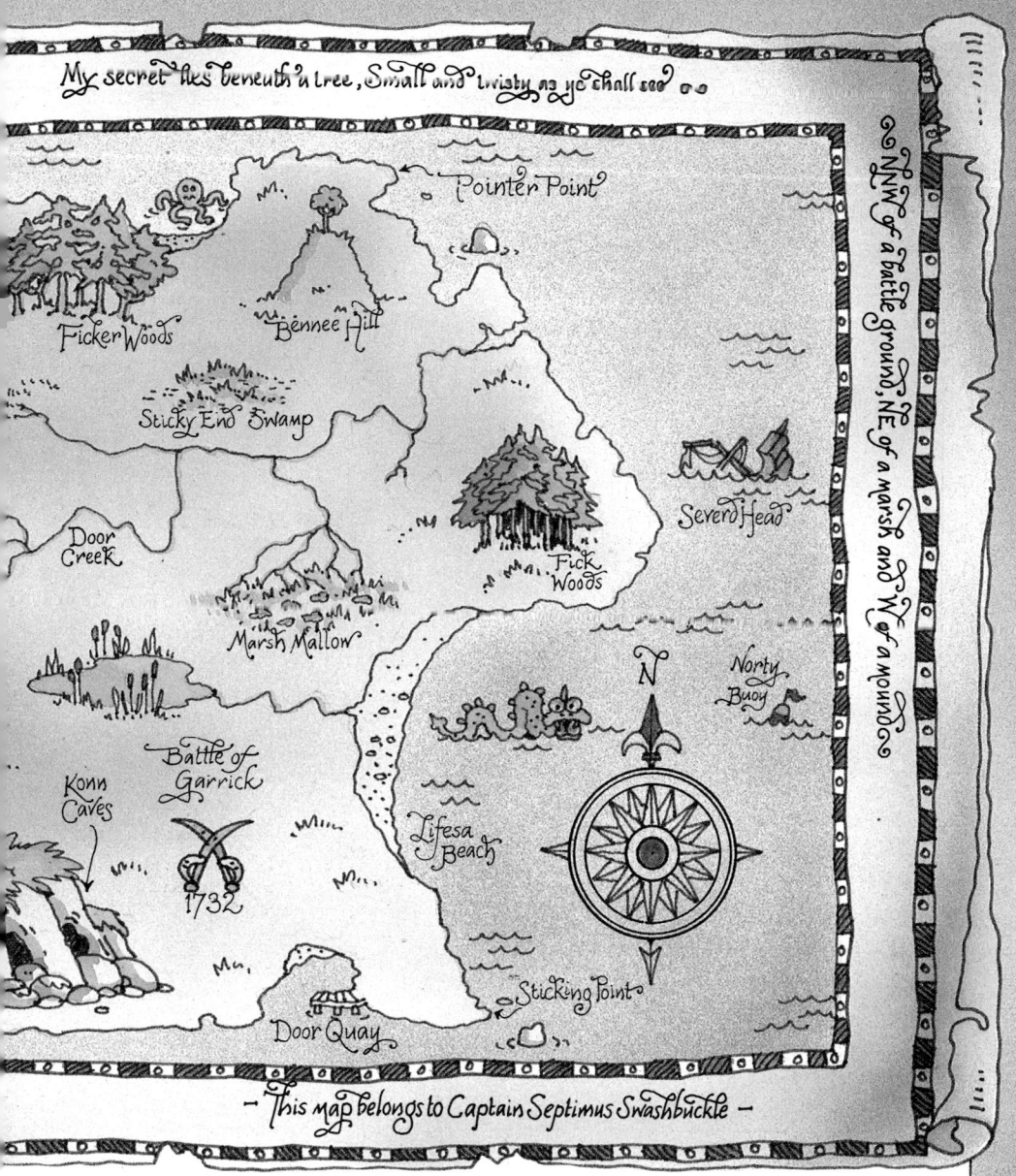

My secret lies beneath a tree, Small and twisty as ye shall see

Pointer Point

Ficker Woods

Bennee Hill

Sticky End Swamp

Door Creek

Marsh Mallow

Konn Caves

Battle of Garrick

1732

Door Quay

Fick Woods

Severd Head

Lifesa Beach

N

Norty Buoy

Sticking Point

NW of a battle ground, NE of a marsh and W of a mound

This map belongs to Captain Septimus Swashbuckle

There wasn't a moment to lose. Fillet and his friends were bound to discover their escape soon and give chase. They studied the map carefully. At first the clues didn't make sense.

Then Charlie realized they were muddled up and began putting them in order.

What do the clues say?
Where do they lead?

Underground Tunnel

They followed the clues to the small, twisted tree and began clearing away the fallen leaves and earth, in search of the trapdoor.

"Here it is," Nic cried, digging up a rusty handle.

She had found the ancient door. It was stiff with age, but they managed to lever it open. Soon they were staring into the dark depths of an underground passage. Warily they stepped in. Their way was lit by the moon shining eerily into the long, winding tunnel.

The path twisted and turned, and the stony ground was hard to walk on. Charlie jumped as something small and furry scuttled across his foot. At long last, the path began to slope steeply upwards and they saw a chink of light shining above them. Scrambling up some stone steps towards it, they found themselves in a small, cold room.

When their eyes adjusted to the dim light they glanced around the room and gasped in amazement. Dusty portraits lined the walls. Charlie thought some of the pictures looked familiar but he couldn't be sure.

Just then Kive spotted a gleam of light coming from a small alcove. He reached in and pulled out . . .

. . . a magnificent golden cup encrusted with jewels. Surely this was Swashbuckle's treasure. Lord Kive could hardly believe his eyes. Nic, Charlie and Ali clustered round for a better look.

"Swashbuckle's long-lost chalice," Kive gasped, carefully examining it. "This is legendary. A priceless historical find . . . and I'm holding it."

No Way Out

Lord Kive beamed with delight as he gazed at the chalice.

"I can never thank you enough for helping me find it," he said.

Nic looked glum. After all their detective work, this didn't seem much like real treasure. She had expected a great hoard of pirate gold, doubloons and pieces of eight. But there was no time to feel disappointed.

"Sshhh," Ali hissed. "There's someone coming this way."

All four listened and heard the unmistakeable voices of Fillet and his friends echoing up from the depths of the tunnel. Before long, they would be here.

In desperation, they searched for another way out, but there was only the tunnel. They were trapped. Then something in one of the paintings caught Ali's eye.

"There's a secret door," she cried. "And I know where it is."

**Where is the secret door?
How do they open it?**

37

Escape from Spectre's Isle

They stepped straight out into the entrance hall.

"That was a narrow escape," said Ali. "But we're safe now."

Just then the door creaked open and Fillet's foot appeared. The gang were right behind them.

Nic took charge as the fishy felons burst through the secret door. There was only one thing they could do.

"Run for it!" she yelled.

The others sprinted after her and dashed out of the tower.

They raced down the hill heading for the shore. Charlie glanced back over his shoulder and gulped. The criminals were still hard on their heels, getting closer every second.

Then Charlie had a brainwave. He kicked a small, round stone towards the pursuing villains. Bream stepped on it and went flying, closely followed by his crooked cronies.

While the fake ghosts untangled themselves, Charlie, Nic, Ali and Kive stumbled down the rough path to the sea front. But when they got there, they looked around in horror. The causeway was under water. Ali spotted a small rubber dinghy, but it was only big enough for one. They were trapped!

The situation was desperate. Nic's brain clunked into gear. She thought back to the ghostly coded message and realized there MUST be another means of escape, if only they could find it.

How can they escape from Spectre's Isle?

Swashbuckle's Last Word

Charlie and Ali quickly dragged the boat across the rocks and lowered it into the sea.

"Let's go," shouted Kive, grabbing the oars.

The villains raced across the beach towards them. Ali waded into the water, pushing the boat out into the shallows.

"Jump aboard," yelled Charlie. "I can fix that creepy crew."

In one swift movement he grabbed a pirate cutlass from the bottom of the boat and plunged it into the rubber dinghy. Ali leapt into the boat as Nic and Kive rowed with all their might away from the shore. The crooks were left floundering behind.

The boat bobbed up and down on the choppy sea. Ali examined the chalice for the first time and found the lid lifted off easily. She peered inside and was amazed to discover a piece of parchment. It was obviously a message from Swashbuckle, but most of it was written in a very strange way. Slowly it began to make sense, except for one thing . . . where was the ruby ring?

What does the message say? Where is the ruby ring?

The Tower

Back at Snoreham, everything happened very quickly. A police boat sped off to pick up the crooks, still on the island.

"Imagine those thugs thinking they could scare us by dressing up and pretending to be pirate ghosts," Charlie scoffed.

With Lord Kive and the chalice safe at the museum, the trio walked along the seafront. They couldn't believe they had found the first clue in Swashbuckle's treasure trail.

As they planned their tropical treasure hunt, Nic looked at the island through the beach binoculars. She could just see Fillet, Bream and Krayfish leaping up and down on the shore.

"Something seems to have frightened them," she said.

Peering closely at the island, the tower looked as dark and mysterious as ever. At once, she saw what had scared the gang.

What has Nic seen?

Clues

Pages 6-7

Look carefully at all the information. What day is it?

Pages 8-9

This is easy. They can jump from rock to rock and use the anchor as a bridge.

Pages 10-11

Try swapping the first word with the second word. Keep going.

Pages 12-13

If the signpost was standing, the sign to the tower would point to the path they have just walked down.

Pages 14-15

Trace the piece of paper and place it over each of the gravestones in turn. Look at the words that appear through the holes.

Pages 16-17

If one cog turns clockwise, the next cog will turn anticlockwise, unless they are connected by a straight rubber band.

Pages 18-19

Trace the tapestry and fit the pieces together. The pictures and words tell a story.

Pages 20-21

Who wins the game of dice? Brian scores 4 with his first throw.

Pages 22-23

This is easy. Use your eyes.

Pages 24-25

Solve the ringed crossword clues. The answers can be rearranged to form a message.

Pages 26-27

Look closely at the people on the Snoreham sea front.

Pages 28-29

This is easier than it looks. Sand is the clue.

Pages 32-33

Try putting the clues in order, using the rhymes as a guideline. Then follow the compass directions carefully.

Pages 36-37

Look closely at everything in the room.

Pages 38-39

Think back to the ghostly message on page 11.

Pages 40-41

Look carefully at the chalice and at Swashbuckle's portrait.

Page 42

Can you see anything strange on the island?

Answers

Pages 6-7

They can cross the causeway at midnight (00.00 hours) tonight.

This is how they work it out: They are told that they can only cross at low tide and when the moon is full. The date is June 21st, the first day of their Snoreham holiday. Nic's diary shows that they will meet Charlie at 4 p.m. and says there is a full moon that night. According to the tidetable the next low tide is at 00.12 hrs on June 22nd, at Great Snoreham. Low tide at Port Snoreham is 12 minutes earlier. This means that the next low tide is at 00.00 hrs, or midnight.

Pages 8-9

The route across the causeway is marked in black.

Pages 10-11

The message is decoded by swapping the first word with the next, and so on. This is what it says:

Friday 4.30. From KK to FF and BB. Go to the graveyard for further information about you know who. Then meet me in the tower at the witching hour. You take the Floating Phantom, and remember to hide it when you get there. PS Ghouls and ghosts awake and let the haunting begin. We may have guests tonight.

Pages 12-13

This is what the signpost would look like if the pieces were fitted together.

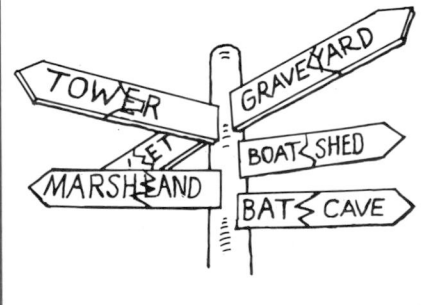

They can find the path to the graveyard by fitting together the pieces of the signpost and standing it up so the tower sign points to the path leading to the tower. All the other signs will then point in the correct directions.

This path leads to the graveyard.

Pages 14-15

When the paper is placed over this gravestone, these words appear through the holes:

TOWER PRISONER WILL DIE SOON.

Pages 16-17

The wheel must be turned anticlockwise to open the door. The arrows show the direction in which each cog turns.

Pages 18-19

SEPTIMUS SWASHBUCKLE, CAPTAIN OF THE PEPPERY CAT, COMMANDER OF A BRAVE BAND OF BUCCANEERS AND BUILDER OF THE TOWER LEADS A LIFE OF ADVENTURE ON THE HIGH SEAS AND AMASSES A HOARD OF

TREASURE AND PRICELESS JEWELS. MORTALLY WOUNDED IN BATTLE HE RETURNS TO HIS TOWER TO DIE AND HERE HE PLANS TO HIDE HIS PRECIOUS HOARD FROM PRYING EYES AND GREEDY HANDS × × × × ×

Hand drawn by Mrs Higgins, Loyal tower-keeper to Captain Swashbuckle, in April 1741.

Pages 20-21

Fred has the highest score. The only possible scores that produce one winner are shown in the table. This means that the ghosts will adopt Fred's strategy. Only the turret room and battlements are safe.

	First throw	Second throw	Total
Brian	4	2	6
Katy	2	4	6
Fred	1	6	7

Pages 22-23

Ali has spotted a copy of the Snoreham News dated June 21st. This proves someone was in the room the previous day. There are several other modern things. These are ringed.

Pages 24-25

Charlie has worked out that the answers to the ringed clues can be rearranged to form this message:

AM TRAPPED IN THE DUNGEON. PLEASE HELP ME AT ONCE, ARCHIVE.

Here is the completed crossword. The answers to the ringed clues are shaded in grey.

Pages 26-27

The imposters are the icecream seller on page 4, the basket maker and the coffee shop waitress, both on page 7. They are called Fred Fillet, Bosun Brian Bream and Katy Krayfish.

Pages 28-29

Nic's plan is to build a mound of sand against the wall, underneath the window. They can then climb up the mound and escape through the window.

Pages 32-33

When the clues are rearranged they form a rhyme:

My secret lies beneath a tree,
Small and twisty as ye shall see.
A door in the ground will show the way,

Which lies NE of a sandy bay.
NNW of a battleground,
NE of a marsh and W of a mound.
Where these points meet there shall be found,
The route to my treasure beneath the ground.

Draw a line from each of the places mentioned, in the compass direction specified. The point where the four lines cross marks the site of the small twisty tree. Underneath this spot is the trapdoor entrance to the secret tunnel leading to the treasure.

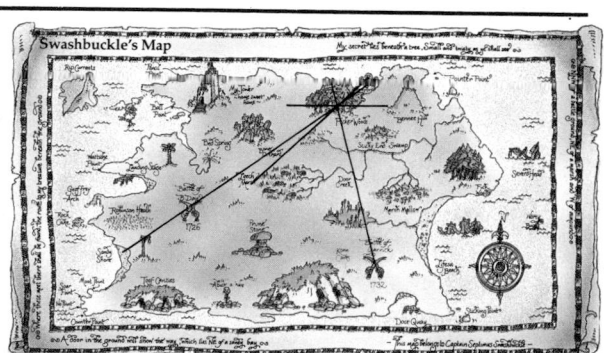

Pages 36-37

You can see a plan of the room in the background of Swashbuckle's portrait. A secret door is marked on it.

The secret door is here.

The rhyme in this book explains how to open the door. This is what it says:

A BUCKLE ON MY SECRET DOOR YOU'LL SEE
PRESS IT HARD AND YOU'LL BE FREE.

Pages 38-39

The message on page 11 mentions the Floating Phantom which is the boat Fred Fillet and Bosun Bream used to cross the island.

The boat is hidden here. They can use it to escape.

Pages 40-41

Part of Swashbuckle's message is written backwards. It says:

My precious hoard lies far from here
Buried in sand by waters clear,
On a tropical island shaped like a bell,
There you must search and all will be well.
For here it is hidden, from here it's retrieved
And not from my tower as most have believed.
If my treasure you seek for unselfish ends
Good luck will befall you, you'll find it my friends.

As long as my ruby ring you possess
Success will be with you during your quest.
Beware and be warned all who start off without it,
My ghost shall haunt ye, forever, don't doubt it.

Here is the ring.

You can see Swashbuckle wearing the ring in the portrait on page 37.

Page 42

Nic has seen a strange white figure . . . the ghost of Captain Swashbuckle?

THE VANISHING VILLAGE

Sarah Dixon

Illustrated by Brenda Haw

Designed by Adrienne Kern

Edited by Karen Dolby

Additional designs by Kim Blundell and Stephen Wright

Contents

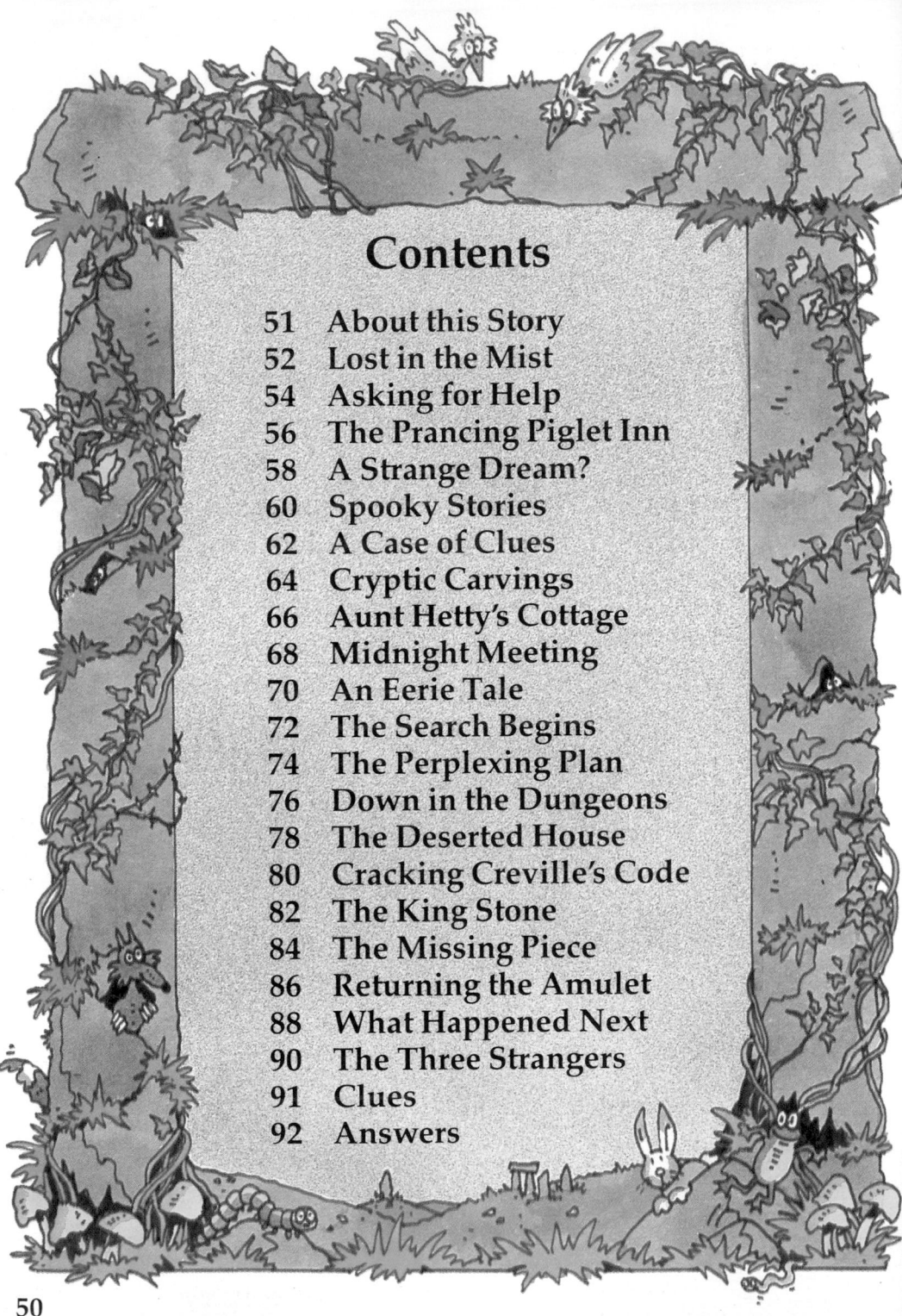

About this Story

The Vanishing Village is a spooky story about a strange village that mysteriously appears at midnight and vanishes without trace by dawn.

Along the way, there are lots of ghostly puzzles and perplexing problems to solve. Find the answers to these before going on to the next episode of the story.

Look at the pictures carefully and watch out for vital clues. Sometimes you will need to flick back through the book to help you find an answer. There are extra clues on page 91 and you can check the answers on pages 92 to 96.

Just turn the page to begin the adventure...

Aunt Hetty

Ben

Jay

Jay and Ben set off to explore the moors around the village of Little Snoozing, where they are staying with Aunt Hetty. She has been telling them ghostly tales about the ruined castles, deserted manor houses and ancient standing stones on the moors.

Lost in the Mist

Jay and Ben stumbled through the rough grass, looking for the path back to Little Snoozing. It was dark and a swirling, purple mist surrounded them. They were cold and lost.

Ben spotted the blurred outlines of stones on top of a hill, just visible through the mist ahead. He dug into his rucksack for his map. There was a dull ripping sound and it fell to pieces in his hands.

"We'll never find our way back now," Jay groaned.

SPLASH! She found herself skidding into a pool of icy water. She squelched back to dry land and yanked off her soggy boots. As she tipped out the water, a strange piece of metal fell out of her left boot.

Suddenly a bell tolled in the distance. One, two, three . . . twelve strokes. Was it really midnight? Jay glanced at her watch but it had stopped. At least the mist was beginning to clear. She saw lights glowing in the valley below. Soon she could even make out the outlines of houses in a village.

**Look at Ben's map.
Can you find the village on it?**

Asking for Help

It was very confusing. The village was in Mourne Valley, but nothing was marked on Ben's map. Feeling cold and tired, they decided to go down to the mysterious village and ask for help.

As they walked along the cobbled streets, a tingling sensation crept down their necks. Jay shivered. There was no one around except for a girl and a pig. When Ben asked her how to get to Little Snoozing, she looked puzzled.

"Ask Harold," she said. "He'll help you. He's the innkeeper at The Prancing Piglet. I'd take you there myself, but I'm in a hurry. You can see the inn from here. It's the half-timbered building with the tiled roof, two chimneys and two attic windows."

Jay and Ben stared at the jumble of roof-tops ahead. Which one was the inn?

Can you find the inn?

The Prancing Piglet Inn

The Prancing Piglet Inn

She must be off to a fancy dress party.

What's the pig going as?

They clattered down the narrow streets towards the inn. Ben tugged a thick rope next to the door and a bell clanged loudly. Immediately, the door opened and a man peered out.

"Come in," he said, smiling. "I'm Harold, the innkeeper."

They followed Harold into a warm, cheerful room with a roaring log fire.

"We're trying to get back to Little Snoozing," Jay explained. "Aunt Hetty will be worried. Can you help us?"

"It's very late and too dark to set off now," Harold said. "You can stay here. I'll make sure your aunt gets a message."

Just then, a boy the same age as Jay and Ben walked in and gave them a friendly grin.

"Could you find these two a room, Thomas?" asked Harold.

Jay was about to protest, but before she could say a word, she began to feel strangely at home in the inn. She was so warm and comfortable in the large wooden armchair by the fire. It would be a long, tiring journey back in the darkness and mist . . . Of course they should stay! She yawned sleepily.

A Strange Dream?

Ben was tucking into a hearty breakfast at The Prancing Piglet and was just about to ask Harold if he could phone Aunt Hetty, when . . . OUCH! He woke up with a jolt. A sharp stone dug into his side. The sun dazzled his eyes. He was outside, back on Bleak Moor. Feeling confused, he shook Jay awake.

"What's happening?" she mumbled, rubbing her eyes. "What are we doing here? Where's Harold and Thomas and the village inn?"

They turned to look down into the valley, but the roof-tops and cobbled streets had vanished. All they could see were trees and more trees. Could they really have imagined it all?

> How weird! It seemed so real – the village, the girl with the pig, the inn, Harold's homemade soup, the comfortable bed . . .

As they tramped through the heather towards Little Snoozing, Jay had a vivid flashback. She was lying in her bed at the inn, half-asleep. In front of her stood a shadowy figure who was trying to tell her something.

"But that sounds just like my dream," Ben gasped, when Jay described what she remembered.

They stared at one another in disbelief. They had both had the same dream – identical, except the figure had said different things. In their dreams, the words had seemed strange and jumbled, but as Jay and Ben repeated them, they realized the words made an eerie message.

What is the message?

Spooky Stories

Back in Little Snoozing, Jay spotted Aunt Hetty disappearing into the Greasy Spoon Cafe.

"Aunt Hetty!" Jay cried, running into the cafe.

"I got your message," Aunt Hetty smiled.

So a message HAD been sent... But who had sent it? Harold? But that meant their night in the village was real. But if the village was real, why had it vanished by the morning?

"How strange," Jay muttered.

"What is?" asked Aunt Hetty.

"Everything," said Ben. "The message and the village and Mourne Valley..."

"Oh, Mourne Valley's strange all right," piped up an old man.

And this started everyone off. There seemed to be hundreds of mysteries and eerie tales about Mourne Valley. Ben looked around, then gasped in amazement. Perhaps some of the tales were true!

What has Ben realized?

There is an old tale about a mysterious village in Mourne Valley that vanished into thin air hundreds of years ago. Of course, no one really believes it.

Little Snoozing ANNUAL JUMBLE SALE 30th April 9–4 in aid of Insomniacs Anonymous

Some say you can hear a ghostly bell in the valley.

Legend says that the ghostly village only appears on the last three nights of the fourth month when the bell tolls twelve times... It's just a story, though

Have you heard the one about the peddlar who found a goblet from the phantom village and claimed he walked into the village that very night?

A Case of Clues

Yawn...

They decided to take Aunt Hetty's advice and go to the museum. They slurped down their milkshakes and set off, determined to find out more about the mystery village.

The museum looked dismally dreary inside. There were no costumes, no suits of armour and no model castles.

Jay peered into the dusty glass cases one by one. King Hengist's stamp collection. The last will of D. Wisp. How boring and useless. Then she spotted a small case tucked away in a dingy corner.

"There used to be a REAL village in Mourne Valley," she exclaimed to Ben, minutes later. "I've even found out its name."

Ben looked blank.

"Remember the villages on your map and the picture in the inn?" she said. "They gave me a clue."

What is the name of the village?

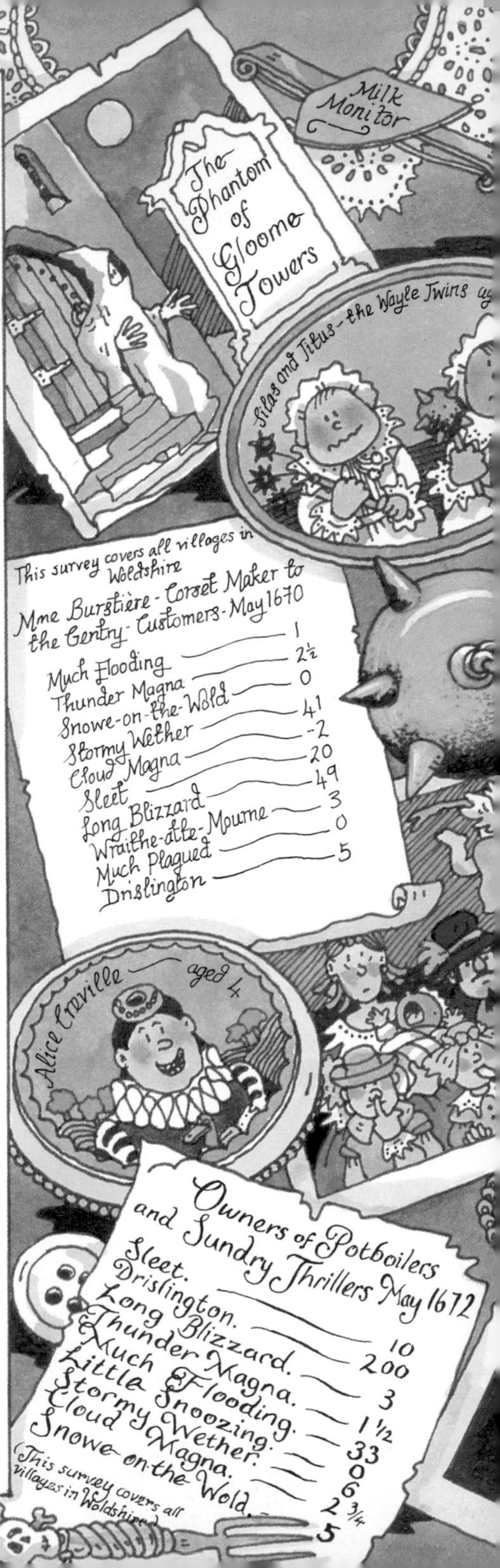

The Phantom of Gloome Towers

Silas and Titus — the Wayle Twins ag

Milk Monitor

Lucky Wishbone

Shopping List
1 partridge pear·
2 call
3 F
4

This survey covers all villages in Weedshire

Mme Burstiere· Corset Maker to the Gentry· Customers· May 1670

Much Flooding	1
Thunder Magna	2½
Snowe-on-the-Wold	0
Stormy Wether	41
Cloud Magna	-2
Sleet	20
Long Blizzard	49
Wraithe-dtte-Mourne	3
Much Plagued	0
Drislington	5

Alice Graville — aged 4

Owners of Potboilers and Sundry Thrillers May 1672

Sleet.	
Drislington.	
Long Blizzard.	10
Thunder Magna.	200
Much Flooding.	3
Little Snoozing.	1½
Stormy Wether.	33
Cloud Magna.	0
Snowe-on-the-Wold.	6
	2¾
	5

(This survey covers all villages in Weldshire)

Will's picklefork

Sir Waldo Raleigh's
Potato Knife.

Henzzer Wayle aged 6

Identity Card
Name — Groan
1615 — Creville's Chef

Identity Card
Name — GRUMBLE
Job — CREVILLE'S butler

Family Crests

The Tenant of Wildmoor Hall | Lord Gloome | Lord Howlingale

Sir Gervaise Creville | Will Chill | Abbot of Crumbledown

Lord Gloome and family at rest — 1677

Readers of Witch Magazine April 1668

1 Much Plagued.
1 Long Blizzard.
0 Drislington.
½ Sleet.
2 Wraithe-atte-Mourne.
1 Much Flooding.
0 Drowne-under-Bleak.
1 Stormy Wether.
4 Little Snoozing.
0 Cloud Magna.
Snowe-on-the-Wold.
Thunder Magna.

This List covers all villages in Woldshire

Lord Crumhorn
alias Red Arrow-highwayman

Hovel and Garden
Subscriptions covering all villages in Woldshire
March 1672

Much Flooding ——— 1
Snowe-on-the-Wold ——— 2
Wraithe-atte-Mourne ——— 10
Cloud Magna ——— ½
Thunder Magna ——— 6
Long Blizzard ——— 7
Little Snoozing ——— 3
Drislington ——— 4
Stormy Wether ——— 0
Sleet ——— 8

Lady Wayle's Beauty Lotion

The Headless Ghost of Wildmoor Castle
— as seen by Claire Vayant

Alice's Toy Duck

(63)

Cryptic Carvings

Ben was amazed. More than three hundred years ago, there had been a village in Mourne Valley, called Wraithe-atte-Mourne. Then suddenly the village had vanished. But how?

As Ben wandered away from the case, he spotted something interesting across the room. He barged past some yawning tourists to take a closer look. It was a sundial from Wraithe-atte-Mourne. Its base was decorated with strange carvings.

"What are they?" Jay asked.

"They're words written in Sombric Script," said the curator, coming up behind them.

She handed them an old book and added, "There's a chapter on Sombric Script in here. It should help you work out what the carvings say".

Ben impatiently flicked through the book. Perhaps the sundial would tell them more about Wraithe.

Can you work out what the carvings say?

64

16th century Sundial from Wraithe-atte-Mourne donated by Dawn Korus

Interesting specimen of

Herbert's wine-making kit

Otto's odds & ends pot

Pots of Fun for everyone

Mug pieces found near Little Snoozing by B. Kerr in 1850

The Mug People

The Mugs lived in Mourne Valley thousands of years ago. They were named after their custom of burying their dead with brightly-coloured mugs and ample supplies of coffee and drinking chocolate to keep them awake during their journey to the underworld.

The Mugs are famous for the standing stones on Sombre Hill (sometimes wrongly called a stone circle). The arrangement of the stones appears jumbled, but they are in fact arranged in 14 rows, running north to south. Each row contains between two and seven stones, and there are large gaps between some of them. There are also four single stones which stand alone in the group. The very famous UFO specialist, Don Vannikin, claims these rows are landing markers for ancient extra-terrestrials and are still regularly used as a refuelling point.

The Mugs told many stories and carved them onto disused standing stones in Sombric Script. In 1888 Sir Diggory Fyndes translated their famous saga, Bare Wilf, from Sombric Script, using his Grid Principle. There are no gaps between words in Sombric Script and numbers are written as upright strokes – 1 is one, 11 is two, etc.

A B C D E F G H I J K L M N
O P Q R S T U V W X Y Z

The Sombric Alphabet

Aunt Hetty's Cottage

Later, back at Aunt Hetty's cottage, Jay and Ben planned their next move. The carvings on the sundial were useless rubbish. Nothing to do with the vanishing village at all!

Jay thought about what the man with the newspaper had said in the cafe. Today was the 30th of April. If the legend was true, that meant tonight was the last time the village would appear this year.

"Let's go back to Mourne Valley tonight and see," she said.

Ben remembered the last words of the cloaked figure, urging them to return. Where would they find an object from the village to take with them?

"The only thing we've seen is that rotten sundial," he sighed. "We can't take that!"

He looked at Jay glumly, then nearly fell off his chair in amazement. Out of the corner of his eye, he caught sight of an object that looked suspiciously like something he had seen in the village inn.

What has Ben spotted?

67

Midnight Meeting

That night, Jay and Ben scrambled through the heather to the pool on the top of Bleak Moor, clutching the silver spoon. In the distance a bell tolled twelve times.

Their hearts pounded as they gazed at Mourne Valley below. Would the village appear again?

"Look!" Ben cried. "Lights... and houses!"

He raced down towards the village with Jay panting behind him. A familiar tingling sensation ran down their necks when they reached the first cottages in the valley.

A maze of winding streets led them past more cottages and a bell tower to a small village square and a river with stepping stones. Jay leapt onto the first stone, then...

"Over here!" hissed a voice.

SPLASH! Jay lost her balance and found herself knee-deep in icy water again. A cloaked figure holding a lantern stood in front of her. It was the person they had seen last night.

"Come with me," the figure said. "We must talk."

Ben hesitated. Who was this mysterious hooded character and what did he want?

Suddenly, Ben caught sight of the figure's face, lit for an instant by the glow from the lantern. He grinned. So that's who it was.

Who is the mysterious figure?

An Eerie Tale

They followed Thomas along an alley and into The Prancing Piglet Inn. Jay pulled off her wet boots and soggy socks, and all three sat down in front of the blazing fire.

"I'm so glad you've come back!" Thomas exclaimed. "The amulet must be found. It's all Creville's fault. We're trapped. We can't do anything. So I had to get you back to release us from the curse. I'm sure the amulet's in Gloome Towers . . ."

"Hang on!" Jay said, confused. "What's the amulet? Who's Creville? What's he done?"

"And what's this curse?" Ben gulped, feeling uneasy.

The room fell silent. Outside, the wind began to howl. Ben shivered. Thomas threw another log on the fire, then he leant forward and began to tell them an eerie tale.

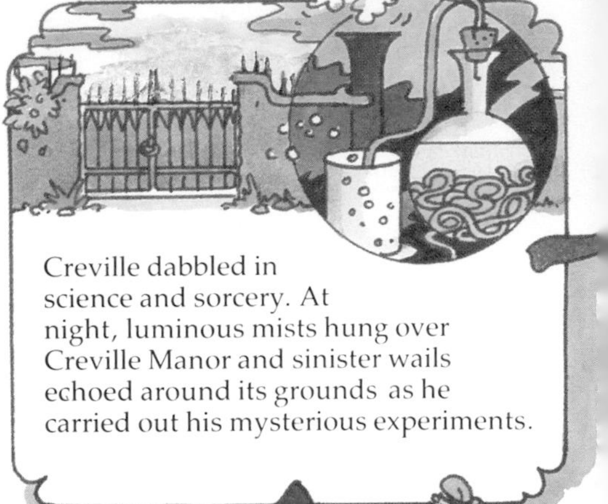

Creville dabbled in science and sorcery. At night, luminous mists hung over Creville Manor and sinister wails echoed around its grounds as he carried out his mysterious experiments.

The local lord of the manor was called Sir Gervaise Creville. He owned our village of Wraithe-atte-Mourne.

Creville
always needed
money to buy peculiar things
like unicorns' horns, griffins' tongues
and dragons' teeth for his weird
experiments, so he sold our crops and
animals, leaving us short of food.

Things went from bad to worse and
finally we went to Creville to beg him
to give us food, or we would starve.
We peered through the locked gates
of Creville Manor.

The next day, the Dragon Amulet, our
magic charm, had disappeared from the
ancient statue in the village square. Next
to the statue lay Creville's ring. He had
stolen the amulet to use in experiments
because it has strange powers...

Suddenly there was a flash of purple
light. Seconds later, Creville's dogs
hurled themselves against the gates,
growling ferociously. We fled back to
the village.

The amulet protects the village from
harm. It is made of an unknown gold
metal, shaped like a dragon. No one
knows where it came from, but it has
always been kept in the statue.
According to legend, the village
vanishes if the amulet is taken away...

And from that day the village has been
shrouded in a timeless mist. Although
we're free from Creville, we are trapped
in eternal limbo and have been waiting
for someone to release us.

The Search Begins

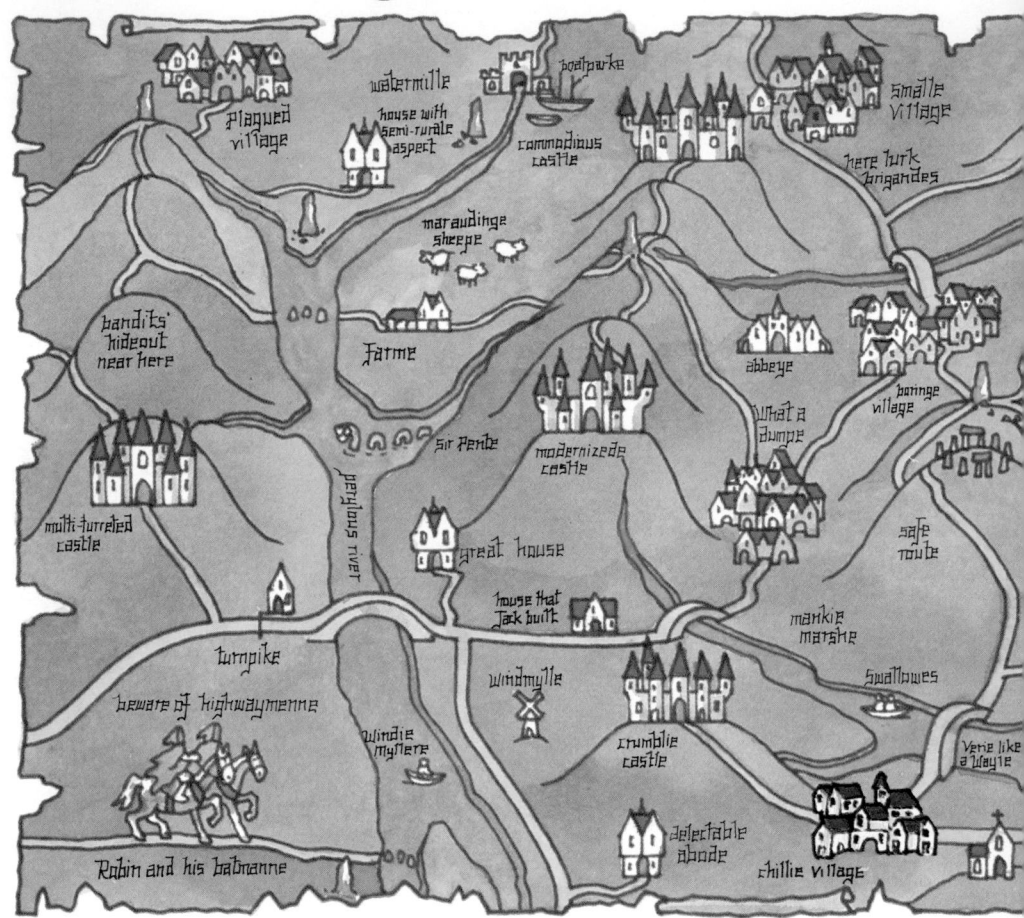

J ay and Ben stared at Thomas, aghast. It was a terrible story. But what could they do to help?

"We need you to find the Dragon Amulet and bring it back to the statue," Thomas explained. "Only then will the village be released from limbo."

"But how are we going to find the amulet?" Jay cried. "It could be anywhere!"

"All we know is that Creville stole it," Thomas said. "He probably took it to his secret laboratory in Red Arrow's cell, hidden deep in the dungeons of Gloome Towers.

"But that was over 300 years ago!" exclaimed Ben. "It won't be there now."

"How do you know?" Thomas asked.

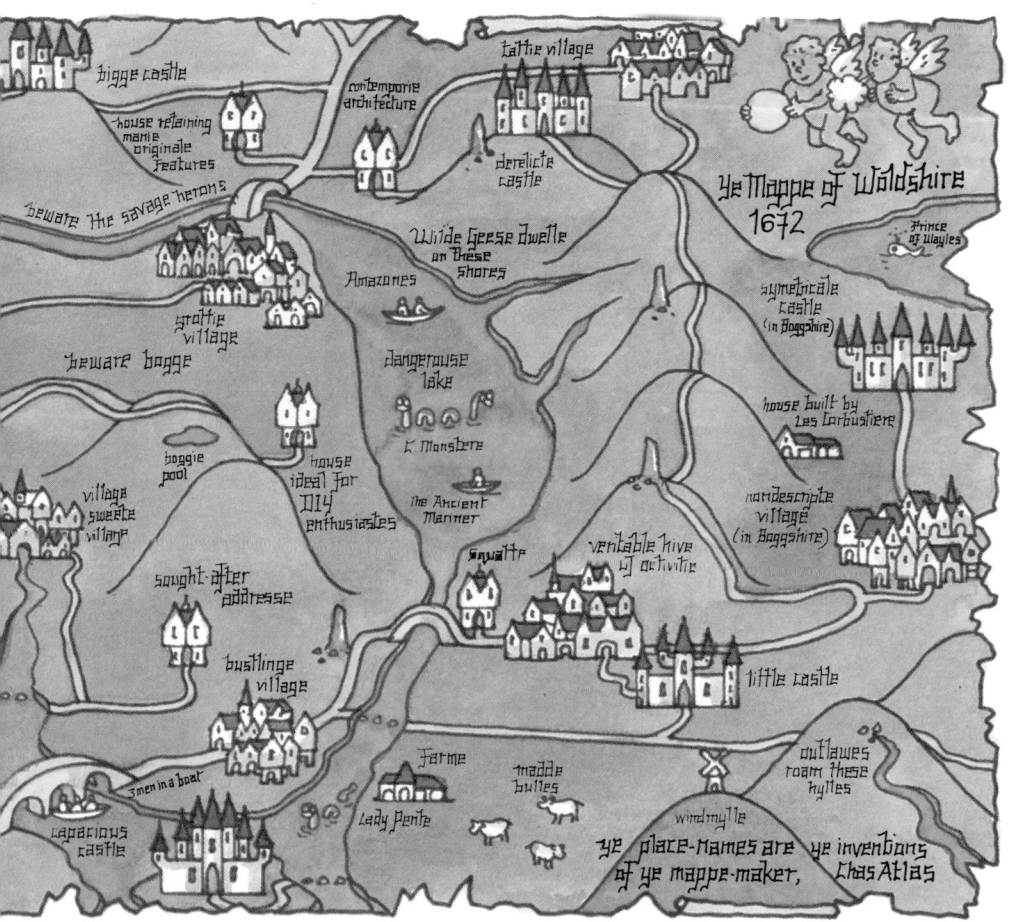

Ye Mappe of Woldshire 1672

bigge castle

house retaining manie originale features

beware the savage herons

grottie village

beware bogge

village sweete village

boggie pool

house ideal for DIY enthusiastes

sought-after addresse

bustlinge village

rapacious castle

3 men in a boat

Lady Pente

Farme

madde bulles

contemporie architecture

tattie village

derelicte castle

Whilde Geese dwelle on these shores

Amazones

dangerouse lake

Y. Monstere

The Ancient Manner

Smallte

veritable hive of activitie

little castle

windmylle

ye place-names are ye inventions of ye mappe-maker, Chas Atlas

Prince of Wlayles

symetricale castle (in Boggshire)

house built by Les Corbustiere

nondescripte village (in Boggshire)

outlawes roam these hylles

Jay and Ben looked doubtful. It WAS their only lead...

"But how do we get back to the village? Tomorrow is the 1st of May," Jay said.

"The village is always here, even if you can't see it," Thomas replied. "When you return to Mourne Valley with the amulet, go to the site of the statue. Then the curse will be lifted."

He unrolled a tattered map and added, "You can see Gloome Towers on here. It's the castle with six turrets."

"That map's ancient," Jay said. "We need to find Gloome Towers on our modern map... if it still exists."

Can you find Gloome Towers on Ben's map?
What is the shortest route there?

The Perplexing Plan

J ay clattered along the cobbled lane out of the village. Ben hurried after her. As he ran past the last houses, he felt the same sharp tingle in his neck that he had noticed before.

Gasping for breath, they scrambled up the steep hill to Bleak Moor. When they reached the top, they looked down into Mourne Valley for one last glimpse of the village.

Suddenly, Ben pointed and cried out in amazement. Even as they watched, the valley was growing darker and mistier . . . the village was vanishing in front of their very eyes!

They raced on across Bleak Moor, leaving Mourne Valley behind, shrouded in darkness. Before long, a ruined castle loomed above them, sinister in the moonlight. This was Gloome Towers, but only one of its six turrets was standing.

Would they still be able to find a way into the dungeons? Jay stared at the heavy turret door. It looked very solid and locked. She grabbed its rusty handle and began to heave and tug. Suddenly the door swung open, sending her flying.

Nervously, Ben peered inside. As his eyes became used to the dark, he could see hundreds of stone steps leading down into the blackness below. On the back of the door hung a tattered piece of parchment. It was a plan of the cells with prisoners' names written on it.

But where was Red Arrow's cell? Ben scanned the plan again and again. Just as he was about to give up hope, a name suddenly caught his eye. Hadn't he seen it in the museum?

**Where is Red Arrow's cell?
How can they get there?**

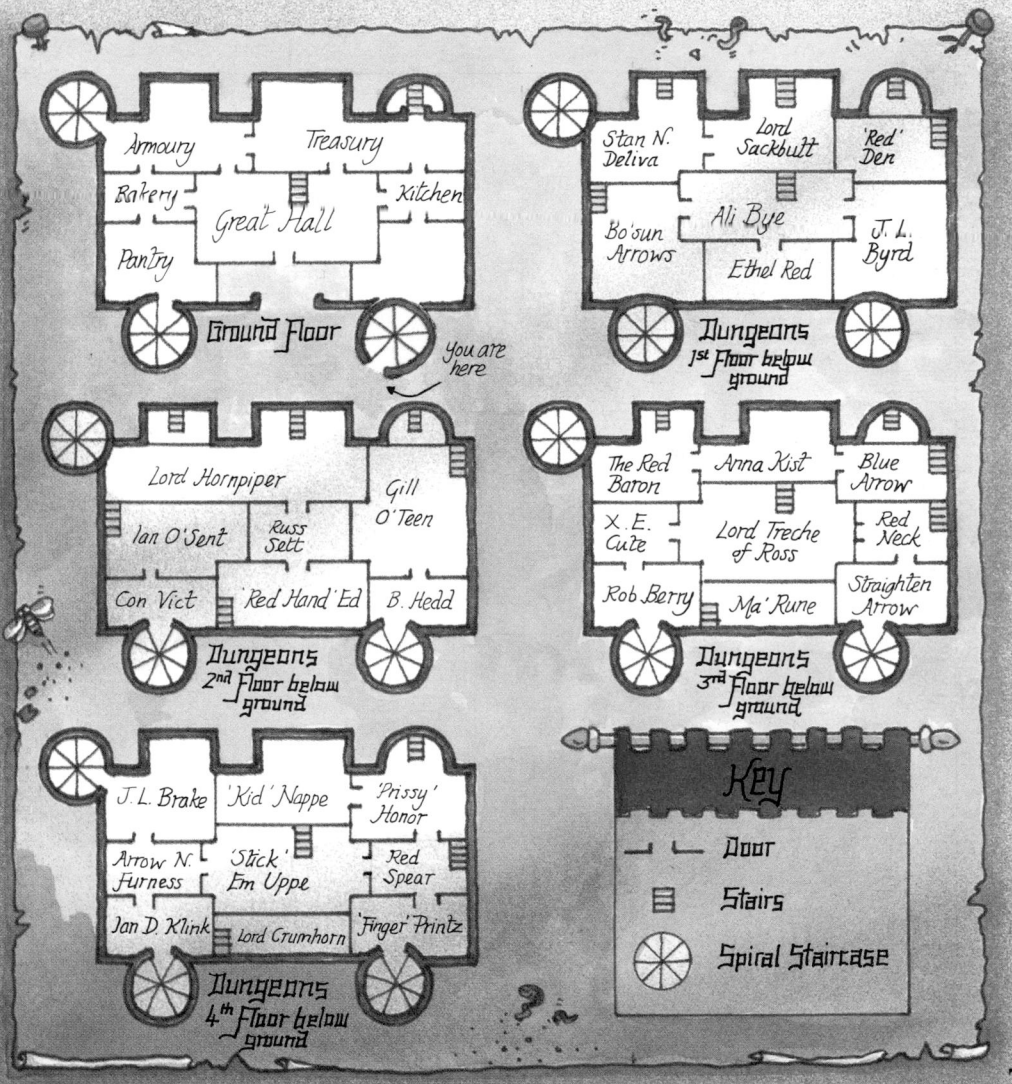

Ground Floor: Armoury, Treasury, Bakery, Great Hall, Kitchen, Pantry
You are here

Dungeons 1st Floor below ground: Stan N. Deliva, Lord Sackbutt, 'Red' Den, Bo'sun Arrows, Ali Bye, J. L. Byrd, Ethel Red

Dungeons 2nd Floor below ground: Lord Hornpiper, Gill O'Teen, Ian O'Sent, Russ Sett, Con Vict, 'Red Hand' Ed, B. Hedd

Dungeons 3rd Floor below ground: The Red Baron, Anna Kist, Blue Arrow, X. E. Cute, Lord Treche of Ross, Red Neck, Rob Berry, Ma' Rune, Straighten Arrow

Dungeons 4th Floor below ground: J. L. Brake, 'Kid' Nappe, 'Prissy' Honor, Arrow N. Furness, 'Stick' Em Uppe, Red Spear, Jan D. Klink, Lord Crumhorn, 'Finger' Printz

KEY
⌐⌐ Door
▤ Stairs
✺ Spiral Staircase

Down in the Dungeons

THUD

They crept gingerly down the steps to the dungeons. Ben shone his torch into the first cell. It looked empty, so he marched confidently inside. Suddenly the air was filled with beating wings and high-pitched squeals.

"Bats!" he shuddered.

They raced into the next cell and down a flight of steps. They ran on through silent, spooky rooms and stumbled up and down slippery stone stairs until they reached Red Arrow's cell.

Jay shivered. The cell was very creepy. Huge cobwebs hung from the ceiling and everything was covered in a thick layer of dust. Now their search for the amulet began. They peered in pots, crawled under the table and looked in gaps in the wall. But as they had feared, it was nowhere to be found.

A gust of wind whistled through the dingy dungeons. Was that laughter? Jay caught her breath, listening hard. An eerie silence followed. Perhaps she was imagining things.

THUD! The sound came from above. Alarmed, Jay and Ben sprinted back up to the turret door. It had jammed shut. They tugged and heaved as hard as they could, but the door wouldn't budge. They looked at one another in horror.

"Come on," said Ben, trying to sound calm. "Let's try to find another way out."

They raced back down to the dungeons and through a maze of cells. Soon Jay felt completely lost. Perhaps they would never find a way out. They could be trapped for ever in the damp, dark dungeons.

Ouch, my toe.

Ben shone his torch ahead but could only see a dead end. There was no way out. He slumped miserably against the wall. With a loud CLICK, a lever sprang shut beneath his right foot. The next second, the wall disappeared and Ben found himself falling backwards. He had discovered another tunnel.

Feeling more hopeful, they followed the passage into a dank room. High above, Ben could see sky. They were at the bottom of a dried-up well.

"We can climb out of here using those ropes and ladders," he said.

Jay was less sure. The ladders had rungs missing and the ropes were old and frayed. But it was their only chance of escape.

Can you find a safe route to the top of the well?

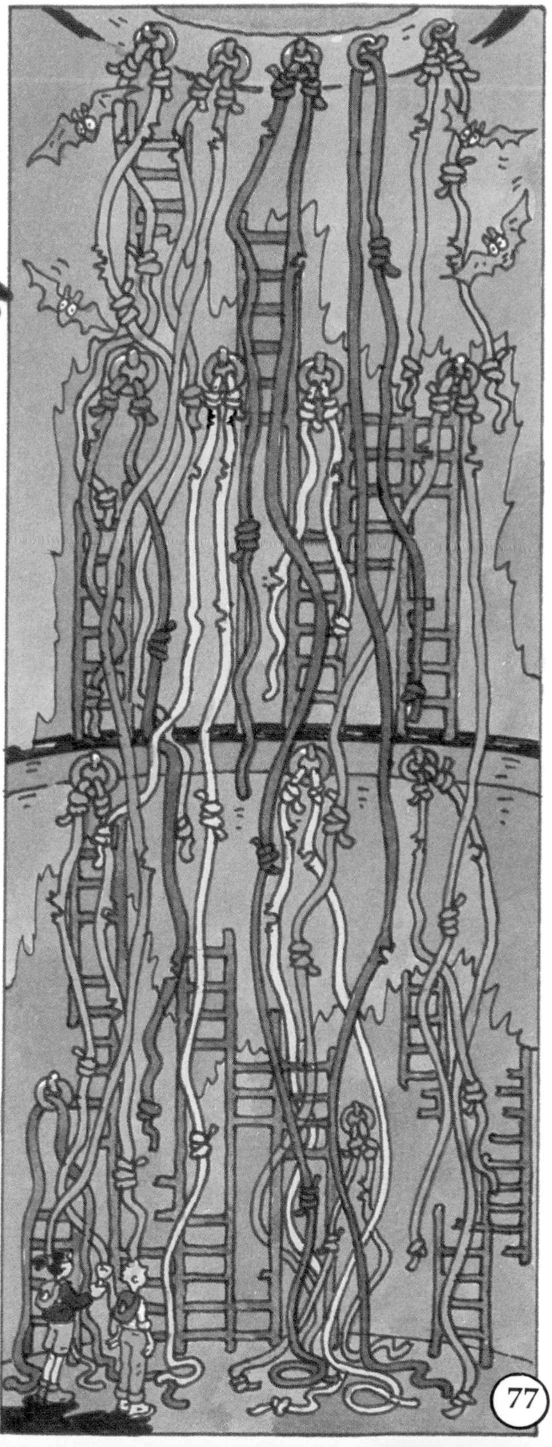

The Deserted House

Jay and Ben clambered out of the well and looked around. They were in the grounds of an old deserted manor house. As Ben gazed up at its sightless windows, he had a strange feeling that someone was watching him. Was that a shadowy figure slipping out of view?

"There's something creepy about this house," he shivered. "Let's get out of here."

"Wait a minute!" hissed Jay.

She stared at a pile of broken statues and crumbling stones in front of the house. The symbols on some of the pieces of stone looked familiar. Then it came to her in a flash. She remembered where she had seen those symbols before and knew where she was.

Where are Jay and Ben?

Cracking Creville's Code

Perhaps the Dragon Amulet was hidden inside Creville Manor. Hundreds of years had passed since Creville lived there. Thomas had said nothing about it being there, but . . .

"We could have a look, just in case," Jay said, as they nervously crept towards the house.

The door creaked open and they stepped inside. When their eyes grew used to the gloom, they realized they were in a large hall.

Jay wandered past the suits of armour, faded tapestries and pewter pots. Then she spotted a book lying on a wooden chest by the window.

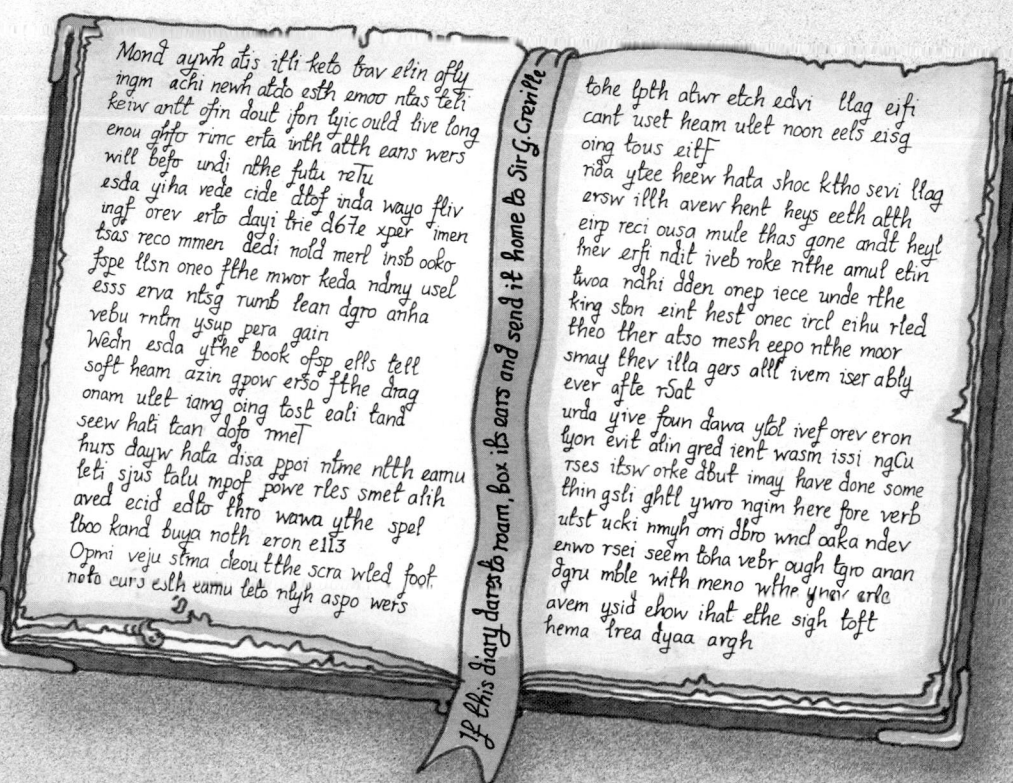

As she blew away the thick layers of dust from its cover, the book fell open at a page covered with spidery writing. But the words made no sense.

"It's Creville's diary," she said, reading the bookmark.

"It might tell us something useful, if we could read it," said Ben, looking over her shoulder.

They stared at the page, baffled. Then Ben realized the writing was in a simple code. Slowly, he began to work out what it said.

BANG! A door slammed somewhere upstairs. An icy draught crept into the hall. Were those footsteps?

Jay and Ben did not stay to find out. They dashed out of the house, across the garden, through the open gates and on into Mourne Valley.

"I know what's happened to the amulet," Ben panted, as he ran. "We've got to go to the stone circle."

What does the diary say?

The King Stone

S oon they were scrambling up the steep hill towards the stone circle. Now they had to find the King Stone and one half of the Dragon Amulet.

Jay stared at the ancient stones. There seemed to be hundreds of them. Some were still upright, while others had toppled over, but there was nothing to show which one was the King Stone.

"This is hopeless," Ben groaned.

"I wonder if the stones have any words or carvings on them," Jay suggested. "Like the . . ."

She stopped, struck by a sudden idea. Of course! The writing on the sundial. They already knew how to find the King Stone.

**The pictures show opposite sides of the big arch in the middle of the stone circle, looking in opposite directions.
Can you spot the King Stone?**

83

The Missing Piece

As soon as they found the King Stone, they began to dig, using sharp pieces of flint and stone. Seconds later, Ben held an oddly-shaped piece of metal in his hand . . . it was half of the amulet.

Jay stared at the piece of amulet, puzzled. It reminded her of something she had seen before. But what? Then she remembered. The first night, lost on the moor . . . the strange metal object in her soggy boot . . .

"I've already found the other half!" she exclaimed.

She fumbled in her rucksack. It HAD to be there. Frantically, she pulled everything out, then gave the bag a last desperate shake. But the amulet had gone.

What could have happened to it? She racked her brains, but it was no use. There was nothing she could do. The missing piece could be anywhere. Now the vanishing village would remain trapped in limbo for ever.

In gloomy silence, they trudged miserably back to Little Snoozing. As she shuffled along the high street, Jay gazed glumly into the shop windows. Garden gnomes, tartan socks, cuddly toys, huge sticks of Little Snoozing rock and . . .

The missing half of the amulet! She stared open-mouthed in disbelief.

Where is the missing piece of the amulet?
How did it get there?

Returning the Amulet

The shopkeeper remembered them from the cafe and gave the piece of amulet back to Jay.

"I thought it was just an old brooch," he smiled. "Ideal for my window display."

"There's no time to lose!" Ben exclaimed, speeding out of the shop. "We've got to get back to Mourne Valley."

When they reached the valley, they found a wood where the village should have been.

"But Wraithe IS still here," said Jay, ducking under a low branch. "We just can't see it."

It was strange to think that they were walking down invisible streets past houses and people. Somewhere among the trees was the site of the statue.

Suddenly Ben heard the sound of rushing water. He pushed through some bushes into a small clearing.

"I'm sure this is the river which ran through the village square," he said. "We must be near the right place now."

The trees by the river looked very old. Ben thought he had seen some of them before.

This gave him an idea. He began drawing imaginary lines between trees and boulders.

"I know where the statue is," he yelled. "Follow me!"

Where should the statue be?

What Happened Next

Clutching the two halves of the Dragon Amulet, they rushed to the spot where the lines met . . . A sharp tingle ran down their necks. The ground shook beneath their feet. In the distance, a bell began to toll. Each stroke sounded nearer and nearer. A clock struck twelve . . .

Jay and Ben blinked, then stared, dazed. They were in a bustling village square. A boy waved as he walked towards them. He looked very familiar.

"What's happened?" Ben gasped. "Who are you?"

"Tom, you idiot," the boy said, puzzled. "Don't you remember?"

"Where are we?" Ben asked.

"In Wraith-at-Mourne, of course," Tom laughed.

"But that's impossible!" Ben exclaimed.

"Why?" said a voice.

Ben turned and saw Aunt Hetty sitting at her easel, smiling at them. As he glanced at the shops around the square, he gaped in disbelief. Wraith was a modern village! It was as if the village had never vanished. But that was impossible – or was it? Could they have changed the course of history when they returned with the amulet?

But where was the amulet? It had disappeared! Had someone stolen it? Would the village vanish again? Jay wandered around for a while, feeling anxious.

Then she smiled. She knew the amulet was safe.

Where is the amulet?

The Three Strangers

Later that day, Tom climbed the steep path to Bleak Moor with Jay and Ben trailing behind. They were off to explore the ruined castle on Wildmoor Hill, which was haunted by a headless woman in green.

"You two are acting very strangely," Tom said. "What's the matter?"

Jay tried to explain about the vanishing village, the amulet and the curse, but Tom just thought it was a good story.

As they reached the top of the moor, Ben spotted three people a little way ahead. He nudged Jay. Hadn't they seen them before?

As the figures came closer, Jay and Ben saw their faces clearly for the first time. They gasped . . .

Then Jay chuckled. She knew who the three strangers were. And she guessed they weren't too pleased. Nothing had worked out quite as they planned.

Who are the three strangers?

Clues

Pages 52-53

This is a trick question. Look on the map for the landmarks in the picture. Don't worry if you can't find the village.

Pages 54-55

This is easy. Use your eyes.

Pages 58-59

Combine the two messages, taking one word from one message and one word from the other, then two words from one and two from the other. Repeat this pattern until you run out of words.

Pages 60-61

Look at the posters. How do they match up with what people are saying?

Pages 62-63

Look carefully at the lists of villages in Woldshire. Most villages appear on all lists, but three do not. What are their names? Look at Ben's map on page 53.

Pages 64-65

Match the carvings on the stone with the symbols in the book.

Pages 66-67

Can you see anything from the inn?

Pages 68-69

He has appeared before.

Pages 72-73

Compare Thomas's map with Ben's map. Can you match up the positions of the rivers and the lake? Gloome Towers could now be a ruin.

Pages 74-75

Does Red Arrow have another name? This is a three-dimensional maze.

Pages 76-77

This is easy, but make sure the ropes are knotted at the top.

Pages 78-79

Some of the pieces have similar markings. Try joining them together. Do you recognize them?

Pages 80-81

The gaps between the words are not in the right places.

Pages 82-83

Look at the description of the standing stones and the carved message on the sundial on page 65. Remember the sun rises in the east.

Pages 84-85

What does the other half of the amulet look like? Turn to page 52 if you can't remember. Then use your eyes.

Pages 86-87

Look at the village square on page 69. Do you recognize any trees or boulders?

Pages 88-89

This is easy if you know what's on in Wraith.

Page 90

Flick back through the book and look at Creville's diary on page 81.

Answers

Pages 52-53

Jay and Ben are standing beside Bleak Pool. This is the only pool on the map so it must be the one Jay fell into. This means they are on Bleak Moor. The picture on page 53 shows the view looking northeast. Through the mist they can see the standing stones on top of Sombre Hill, the ruin on Gale Edge and the small river that runs into River Mourne. The village is in Mourne Valley but it is not marked on the map. The mystery begins...

Jay and Ben are here   The village is here

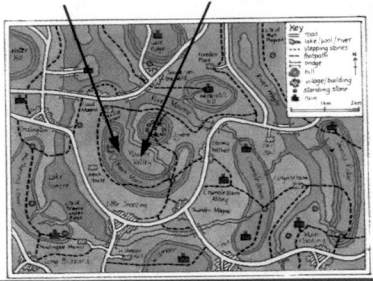

Pages 54-55

This is The Prancing Piglet Inn. ——————

Pages 58-59

The words from both messages must be fitted together to work out what the complete message says. Take one word from Jay's message, then one from Ben's, followed by two words from Jay's and two from Ben's. Follow this pattern of one word followed by two words from each message (always taking the words in the order they appear), until you run out of words.

This is what the complete message says:

We need your help. The ancient curse has taken its terrible revenge. Our village has vanished and we are trapped in eternal limbo. Only you can release us. Please come back to us and I will explain everything. But remember that you must bring something from the village with you.

Pages 60-61

The old man with the white beard says there is an old tale of a mysterious village in Mourne Valley. This was the site of the village that Jay and Ben visited last night. Ben has seen the poster advertizing a jumble sale on the 30th of April. When he hears the man in the checked waistcoat say he is going to the jumble sale, Ben realizes the 30th of April is today.

According to the man with the newspaper, the ghostly village appears only on "the last three days of the fourth month", in other words, the 28th, 29th and 30th of April. Jay and Ben saw the village in Mourne Valley last night, the 29th of April. Perhaps the old tales could be true. If so, the village should appear again tonight for the last time this year.

Pages 62-63

Jay discovers the name of the village in Mourne Valley by looking at the lists. The name of every village on these lists appears on Ben's map, except Wraithe-atte-Mourne.

Wraithe-atte-Mourne appears for the last time on the list dated March 1672. It is not marked on the list dated May 1672. Since the lists cover ALL the villages in Woldshire, this must mean that Wraithe-atte-Mourne no longer exists in May 1672.

The lists do not say where Wraithe-atte-Mourne was, but Jay remembers a picture on the wall of the inn on page 57 showing "The Village in Mourne Valley", dated March 1672. From this, she deduces that Wraithe-atte-Mourne, the village that vanished from the lists, is the village in Mourne Valley.

It looks as though Wraithe-atte-Mourne is the village that appeared in Mourne Valley last night.

Pages 64-65

The symbols on the sundial stand for letters, numbers and full stops, but there are no gaps between words. This is what the inscription on the sundial says with punctuation and word spaces added:

Bare Wilf stood on the hillside and looked eastwards. He walked to the lone sentry stone on the south-west edge of the stones. Then he walked in a straight line due east, passing a row of 7 stones, 2 rows of 4 stones, a row of 5 stones and the lone ranger stone. Then he reached another row of 5 stones. He climbed over the southernmost stone, then passed a row of 3 stones. Next, he walked northwards for a short way up to the queen stone that stands in a row by itself. Turning east again, he stood right in front of the king stone. He sprinkled it with the magic water. Instantly the spell was broken. The king thanked Bare Wilf and gave him all his mugs.

Pages 66-67

Ben has spotted a silver spoon which he recognizes from The Prancing Piglet Inn.

Here it is.

Pages 68-69

The figure is Thomas, the boy they met in the inn on pages 56 and 57.

Pages 72-73

On the map there is a note saying that the names of places are not real but are inventions of the map maker. The only castle with six turrets is "crumblie castle". This must be Gloome Towers.

You can match up Thomas's and Ben's maps by comparing the positions of the lake, rivers, villages and other landmarks, although finding out where hills are is trickier, as the two maps show hills in different ways. By doing this, you can locate the position of Gloome Towers as the ruin on Wetterstill Hill.

When Jay and Ben leave the village, they will return to the present and must use Ben's map to find their way to Gloome Towers. The route is marked in black.

Gloome Towers

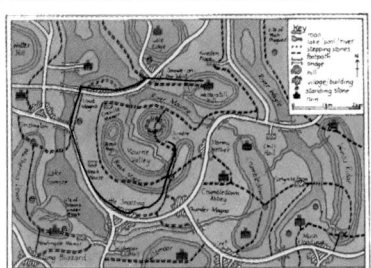

Pages 74-75

Red Arrow is Lord Crumhorn (see page 63). To reach his cell, they first go down the turret stairs to the second floor of the dungeons and then they go through the cells as numbered here.

Start here

Lord Crumhorn's cell

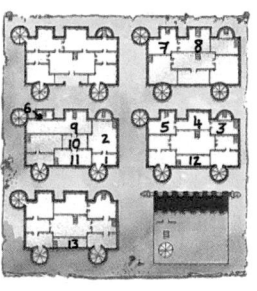

Pages 76-77

The safe route is marked in black.

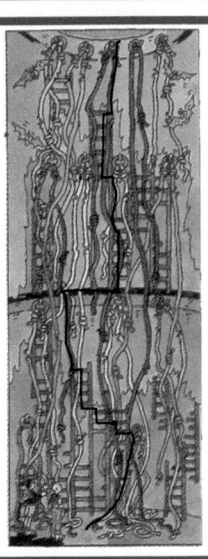

Pages 78-79

Jay has spotted broken pieces of Sir Gervaise Creville's crest, which she saw in the museum on page 63. The crest has crumbled away from the wall above the door. They are in the grounds of Creville Manor, Creville's home.

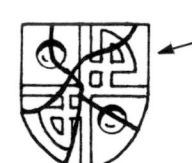

Here is the crest when it is pieced together.

Pages 80-81

The gaps between the words in the diary have been removed and the letters have been divided into groups of four. This is what the diary says with the gaps between the words put in the right places and punctuation added:

Monday: What is it like to travel in a flying machine? What does the moon taste like? I want to find out. If only I could live long enough – for I'm certain that the answers will be found in the future.

Tuesday: I have decided to find a way of living for ever. Today I tried 67 experiments, as recommended in Old Merlin's Book of Spells. None of them worked. And my useless servants, Grumble and Groan, have burnt my supper again.

Wednesday: The Book of Spells tells of the amazing powers of the Dragon Amulet. I am going to steal it and see what it can do for me.

Thursday: What a disappointment. The amulet is just a lump of powerless metal. I have decided to throw away the spell book and buy another one.

11.30 pm: I've just made out the scrawled footnote. Curses! The amulet only has powers to help that wretched village. If I can't use the amulet, no one else is going to use it.

Friday: Tee hee! What a shock those villagers will have when they see that their precious amulet has gone. And they'll never find it – I've broken the amulet in two and hidden one piece under the King Stone in the stone circle. I hurled the other at some sheep on the moors. May the villagers all live miserably ever after.

Saturday: I've found a way to live for ever. Only one vital ingredient was missing.

Curses! It's worked, but I may have done something slightly wrong. I'm here for ever, but stuck in my horrid brown cloak, and, even worse, I seem to have brought Groan and Grumble with me. Now they never leave my side. How I hate the sight of them already! Aaaargh!

Pages 82-83

The inscription on the sundial on page 65 tells them how to find the King Stone.

Their route to the King Stone is marked in red.

The book on page 65 says that the stones are arranged in rows running north to south. Each stone in the first row mentioned in the inscription (a row of seven stones) is marked with an asterisk.

The Sentry Stone

Two stones make up this arch.

The Lone Ranger Stone

The rising sun in the east

The Queen Stone

The King Stone

The route goes behind this stone.

Pages 84-85

Here is the missing piece of the amulet.

The shopkeeper picked it up in the cafe on page 61, where it fell out of Jay's rucksack.

Pages 86-87

Ben remembers that the statue stood in the centre of the village square (see page 69). He recognizes six landmarks that bordered the square. He can locate the statue's position by drawing lines between the six landmarks as shown:

Chestnut tree

Stone

Stepping stone

The statue should be here

Tree stump

Holly bush

Oak tree

Pages 88-89

The poster on the notice board shows that the Dragon Amulet is in Wraith Museum.

Page 90

The three strangers are Sir Gervaise Creville and his servants, Grumble and Groan. Jay and Ben recognize Creville from his portrait on page 56, and Grumble and Groan from their identity cards in the museum on page 63.

Remembering Creville's diary on page 81, Jay knows that Creville cast a spell to make him live for ever but his plans went slightly wrong. He has to wear his horrid cloak and his hated servants, Grumble and Groan, will never leave his side. This may explain his grumpy expression.

THE GHOST IN THE MIRROR

Karen Dolby

Illustrated by Brenda Haw

Designed by Kim Blundell and Brian Robertson

Contents

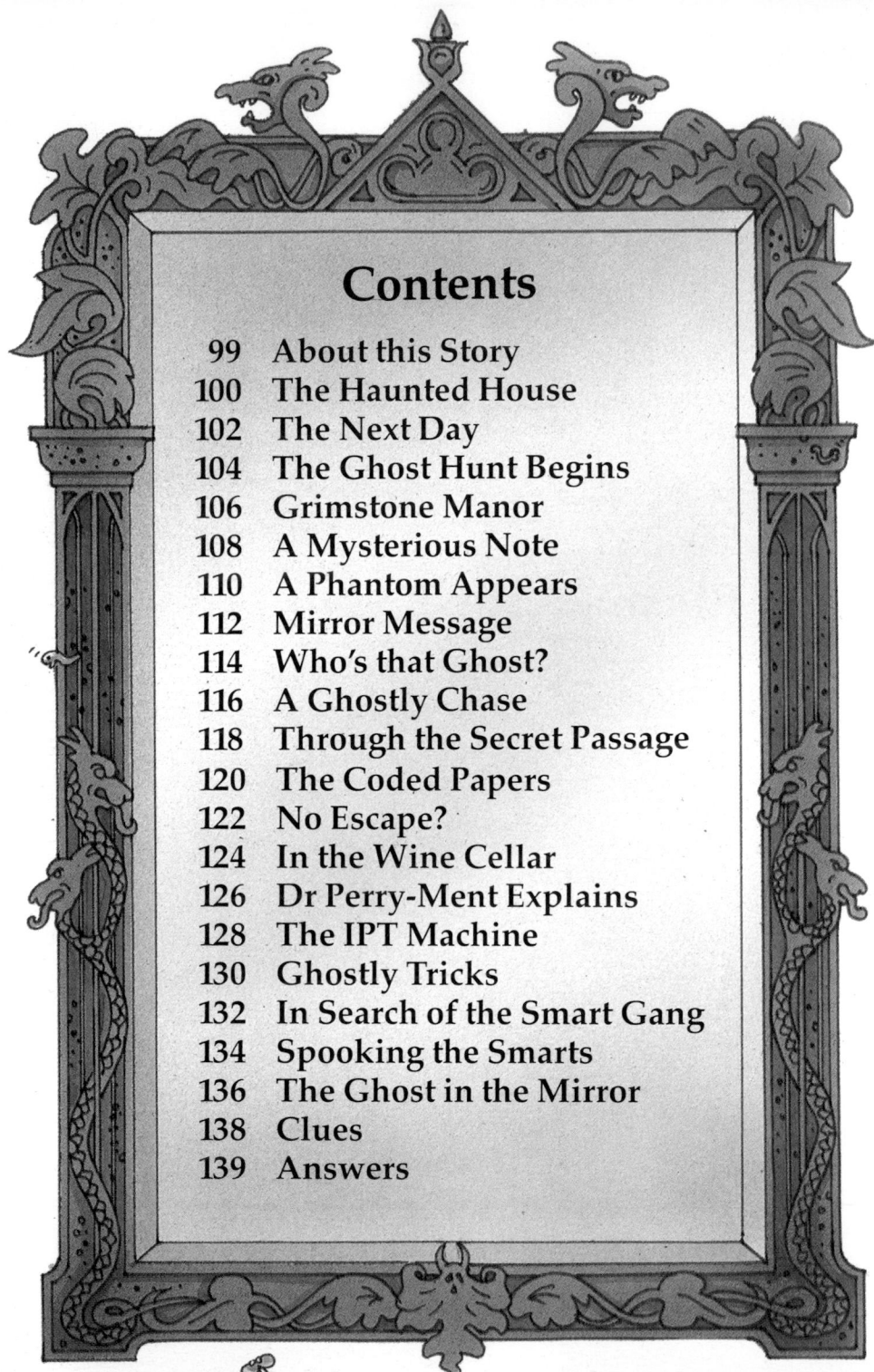

About this Story

The Ghost in the Mirror is a spooky adventure story that takes you on a ghost hunt through a creepy, deserted old manor house.

Along the way, there are lots of ghostly puzzles and perplexing problems to solve. Find the answers to these before going on to the next episode of the story.

Look at the pictures carefully and watch out for vital clues. Sometimes you will need to flick back through the book to help you find an answer. There are extra clues on page 138 and you can check your answers on pages 139 to 144.

Just turn the page to begin the adventure.

Sam, Joe and Polly were on their way home from school late one Friday evening. The gates to Grimstone Park were always locked, but this evening the gates are open. Should they go in? Sam leads the way . . .

GRIM STONE PARK

Joe

Polly

Sam

The Haunted House

Joe, Polly and Sam scuffed their way through the park, drawing closer and closer to Grimstone Manor. The house loomed dark and menacing above the trees.

"Here's the haunted house," Sam joked.

Joe peered through the gates. He had never been so close to the Manor before. Suddenly, an eerie green light glowed through one of the windows. Sam froze in horror as a flickering shadow appeared briefly at the window.

"There's probably someone living there now," Polly gulped.

"But the house has been empty for years," said Sam.

KEEP OUT

An owl hooted suddenly. Polly shivered. Grimstone Manor looked very mysterious. Sam's teeth chattered. He was convinced the house was haunted. But Joe was sure there was another explanation and wanted to investigate.

He stared up at the Manor. It was dark and creepy; the gates were locked; they didn't even have a torch. Perhaps it wasn't such a good idea.

"We'll come back first thing tomorrow," he said, finally.

The Next Day

Joe led the way back to Grimstone Manor, itching to begin the ghost hunt. Sam and Polly followed, struggling to keep up.

"Hide!" Joe whispered suddenly.

He pointed at two odd-looking people lounging against the wall ahead, talking in low voices. He didn't want anyone to see them sneaking around the house.

As they ducked behind some bushes, Sam tripped and dived head first through a small hole in the wall.

Polly and Joe crawled through after him and found themselves staring up at Grimstone Manor. In the daylight it looked empty and neglected and not at all scary. Joe marched up to one of the roughly boarded windows and tugged hard at a sheet of corrugated iron.

He quickly tried the others and groaned. They were securely nailed down and windows that had been left unboarded, were blocked by rubble. He stared at the house and in a flash, saw how they could get in.

Can you find a way in?

The Ghost Hunt Begins

Polly and Joe were soon inside. Sam had more trouble. Joe looped one end of the rope around the bannister rail and pulled. Sam grabbed the pole and Polly tried to haul him in. But Sam remained outside, dangling in midair. He was stuck between the two halves of the window and didn't dare look down.

At last they succeeded. Sam fell in and landed with a bump. He began to wonder if a ghost hunt was worth so much effort. But Joe was already thinking about where to start. It was a large, rambling house. How would they find their way around? The stairs going up were rotten and had collapsed, so they had no choice but to go down first.

Polly and Joe stared through the open door at a crumbling, cobwebby room which used to be a gift shop. The house had been open to the public once.

"It looks as if no one's been here for years," said Polly, venturing inside.

Suddenly she saw something that would be very helpful.

What has Polly spotted?

DINING-ROOM/GIFT SHOP

CRAFTS

LOCAL POTTERY

105

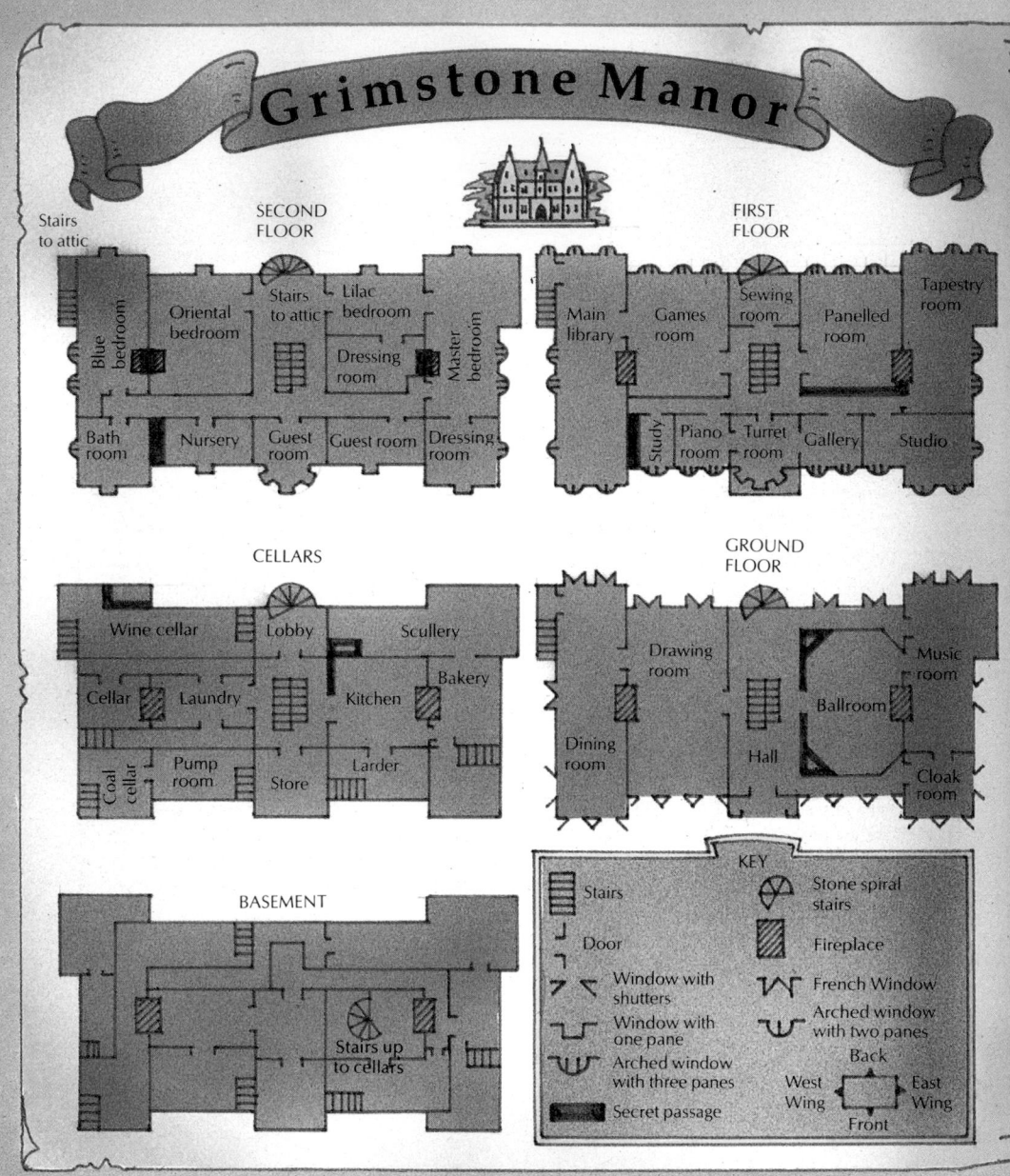

Grimstone Manor

SECOND FLOOR

Stairs to attic

Blue bedroom · Oriental bedroom · Stairs to attic · Lilac bedroom · Dressing room · Master bedroom

Bath room · Nursery · Guest room · Guest room · Dressing room

FIRST FLOOR

Main library · Games room · Sewing room · Panelled room · Tapestry room

Study · Piano room · Turret room · Gallery · Studio

CELLARS

Wine cellar · Lobby · Scullery

Cellar · Laundry · Kitchen · Bakery

Coal cellar · Pump room · Store · Larder

GROUND FLOOR

Drawing room · Music room

Dining room · Hall · Ballroom · Cloak room

BASEMENT

Stairs up to cellars

KEY

Stairs		Stone spiral stairs	
Door		Fireplace	
Window with shutters		French Window	
Window with one pane		Arched window with two panes	
Arched window with three panes			
Secret passage			

West Wing · Back · East Wing · Front

S am read the short history of Grimstone Manor, shivering at the thought of strange lights, ghostly monks and secret passages.

He glanced around nervously expecting a ghastly spectre to appear at any minute.

"Where shall we go?" he asked.

Owners of Grimstone Manor

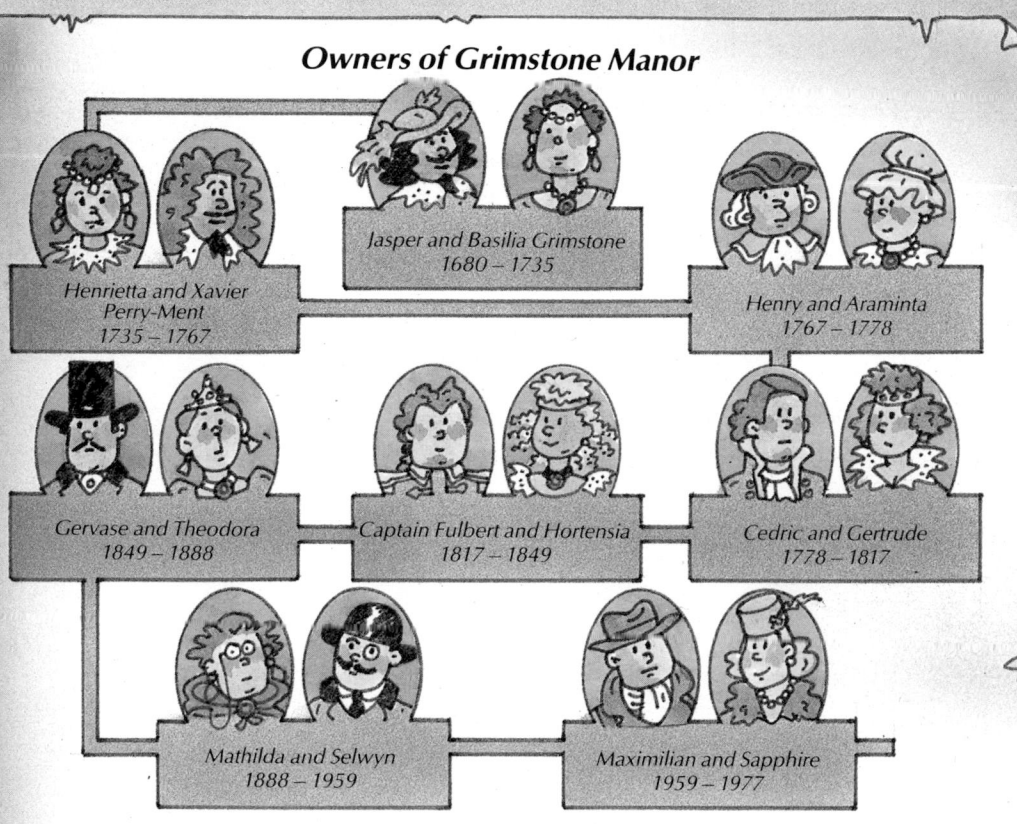

Jasper and Basilia Grimstone 1680 – 1735

Henrietta and Xavier Perry-Ment 1735 – 1767

Henry and Araminta 1767 – 1778

Gervase and Theodora 1849 – 1888

Captain Fulbert and Hortensia 1817 – 1849

Cedric and Gertrude 1778 – 1817

Mathilda and Selwyn 1888 – 1959

Maximilian and Sapphire 1959 – 1977

Grimstone Manor was built in 1680 by Jasper Grimstone. His only daughter, Henrietta, and her husband, Xavier Perrier-Mente, inherited the Manor in 1735. From that time, the house has been owned by the Perry-Ment family who have been known as the Counts and Countesses of Grimstone, since Captain Fulbert won the title for outstanding bravery. An inventive streak has always run through the Perry-Ments. While experimenting with gunpowder in 1862, Gervase blew up the East Wing and ballroom. These were later rebuilt by the brilliant architects, Sir John Truckbrugh and Sir Nicholas Hawksless.

The building itself is very mysterious. The thick walls hide secret passages and small rooms. There are also several secret and well-hidden doors with tricky, mechanical locks.

The Manor has more than its share of ghosts. It is supposed to be built on the site of a medieval priory and is said to be haunted by a spectral monk whose appearance is linked to strange, flashing lights. Visitors to the house have complained of sudden icy breezes, spooky noises and ghostly laughter.

"To the room with the flashing lights, of course," said Polly.

She studied the floor plans and thought back to last night.

She tried to picture the front of the house and soon knew exactly where they had to go.

Which room should they go to?

A Mysterious Note

When they reached the study, the heavy door creaked open. Polly, Joe and Sam peered in uncertainly wondering what to expect.

"Someone's been in here," said Polly, pointing at the thick dust on the floor. "Ghosts don't leave footprints."

Feeling bolder, they began looking around. The room was disappointingly normal and there was no trace of anything ghostly.

It was hard to imagine the strange, glowing light and mysterious, shadowy figure they had seen from outside.

Sam picked up a curious-looking book lying on the armchair and flicked through. It was very old.

"'Ancient Scientific Experiments that didn't Work'," he said, reading the title aloud.

As Joe glanced at the book, something else caught his eye.

Next to a dusty pile of books on the desk was a sheet of paper from a notebook. It was covered with writing and at first Joe thought it was written in a strange language. But as he looked more closely, he realized it was in code.

Can you decode the writing?

Rebmemer
ssap lliw uoy neht dna
elcric eht no sguj eht
ecalp ssalg a yb elttob a
ton elttob a no ssalg a
erom on teg lliw uoy
ro nwod thgir hsup
rood eht rof sserp dna
enilw eht rof sserp
reillem eht tuo ekat
dna selttob eht rof kool
rallec terces ym ot
krad eht morf og ot

A Phantom Appears

Even decoded, the note didn't make any sense. It was definitely human, but it just added to the mystery.

Joe looked up, gulped and grabbed Polly's arm.

"Look…" he gasped, turning a strange colour.

There, in the mirror was a terrible, ghostly apparition. Its face was shrouded, but Sam was sure it was staring at him.

"Let me out of here," he yelled, petrified.

A sudden, icy blast whistled through the room.

SLAM. Sam reached the door as it banged shut. There was a loud click and the latch dropped down on the other side, securely locking the door.

They were trapped in a haunted room. Polly stared into the mirror. The ghost had vanished, but who knew when it might return?

Sam hollered and tugged at the door, but it was no use. Joe rushed to the window. Feeling silly, he realized they were too high up to jump.

Meanwhile, Polly was thinking hard. There was something very peculiar about the large footprints on the dusty floor. They went in one direction only. The more she thought, the more sure she was.

"There's a secret door," she exclaimed, at last. "I know how we can get out."

**Where is the secret door?
How can they open it?**

111

Mirror Message

The bookcase swung open just like a normal door, revealing a flight of stone steps going up. They ran to a small landing at the top and Joe cautiously pulled the red lever in front of him. A panel halfway up the wall slid aside and they clambered out into an old nursery.

Polly rubbed her eyes. The wooden horse in the middle of the room was rocking to and fro.

"There must be a draught," she muttered.

Sam wasn't sure, but he thought the door opposite had just closed quietly. And weren't those footsteps fading into the distance? He jumped as laughter echoed around the house.

"It's the wind," said Joe, sensibly.

Just then, Sam shrieked and made a dash for the door. He had caught sight of a mirror. There was something in it...

"Come back," called Polly. "It's only writing."

Joe was already studying the mirror. He could see the outline of words written in the cobwebby dust, but they didn't seem to make any sense.

"It's another code," exclaimed Polly.

What is written on the mirror?

Who's that Ghost?

Let's look down here.

It was very puzzling. The note in the study and the mirror message were definitely NOT ghostly, but what about the figure in the mirror and the strange noises? And what about the creepy feeling they each had that they were being watched? As they stepped out into the corridor, the nursery door slammed shut behind them.

"I wonder what we'll find?" Polly said, nervously.

Almost before she finished speaking, she heard a low, wailing sound. It grew louder and louder, and closer and closer. Finally, a white, shrouded figure appeared, blocking the corridor ahead. It seemed to float towards them, howling horribly.

"It's the phantom!" Sam yelled.

Polly's knees turned to jelly, but Joe wasn't scared.

"You're no ghost," he shouted. "You don't frighten me."

**Is Joe right?
What has he seen?**

A Ghostly Chase

Joe dashed after the imposter with Polly and Sam hot on his heels. They skidded around a corner in time to see the ghost nipping into a doorway ahead. They ran into a large bedroom after him and stopped. Where was the ghost? Polly looked under the bed, while Joe checked a chest and Sam peered into an enormous wardrobe.

"Over here," he shouted. "It's a door to the next room."

The three climbed through the deep, empty wardrobe into a small bedroom. The white figure glanced back at them and made a hasty exit. Joe, Polly and Sam raced after him and saw the ghost trip over his sheet and fall downstairs.

They followed the ghost into a small room. This time he was trapped. There was nowhere to hide. Suddenly, they were plunged into darkness. Polly flicked on her pocket torch, but the ghost had vanished.

"How did he do that?" asked Sam. "We were blocking the door."

"There must be another secret door," said Polly. "But where?"

Polly thought hard. She was sure something was different. But what was it? If only she knew, it might give them a clue.

What is different?
Where is the secret door?

Through the Secret Passage

Polly had a hunch. She tugged at the silk bell pull, sure it would open the panel. They watched open-mouthed as the fireplace and part of the wall began turning slowly. Halfway round they saw the other, almost identical fireplace swinging into the room.

"Come on," Joe shouted, jumping onto the grate.

The fireplace jolted to a stop in a wide passage. Joe briskly led the way forward. Polly held the torch.

There were strange scuttling noises, loud dripping and their footsteps echoed loudly. Every sound was magnified and it was also very dark. Their torch beam barely pierced the blackness as they crept gingerly down a flight of slippery, stone steps.

"I don't like this," groaned Sam, fighting his way through a cobweb with a rat scuttling across one foot.

Polly had to admit she was feeling a bit spooked and even Joe jumped when he came face to face with a glowing skull leering horribly at him. Finally, they stumbled down a second flight of steps into a narrow bedroom.

There was no sign of the ghost, but there were two small pinpoints of light halfway up the wall. Joe took the first turn to look through the spyholes and peered into a kitchen. He gulped, scarcely believing his eyes.

In a dusty, mirror, he saw the ghostly figure from the study. It seemed to stare through him. He could have been mistaken, but before it faded away, Joe was sure it made a sign as if warning him to be quiet.

The Boss will be pleased with the plan we've stolen.

Mmm… But we've still got to find the Doc and his secret laboratory, Rex.

Immediately, two people walked into the kitchen and Sam replaced Joe. He frowned as he heard snippets of their conversation. What were they up to?

We've seen that girl before," Polly gasped, taking her turn at the spyholes. "But where?"

Where have they seen the girl?

The Coded Papers

As soon as the sinister duo had gone, Sam yanked an old white lever high up in a beam. There was a loud CLICK. A panel sprang open and promptly shut as they climbed through.

"Look," said Polly, running into the room. "They've left this behind."

An official-looking file was lying on the table. Feeling a bit guilty, and making sure they really were alone, they quickly opened it.

Inside, there were two typed sheets, masses of photographs of the same person and a yellow, blue-print plan.

"This might tell us what's going on," said Joe, "… if only we could read it."

Most of the writing was in an impossible-looking code. Polly scratched her head and studied the words. Perhaps it wasn't so tricky after all.

Can you decode the writing?

No Escape?

S am, Joe and Polly flicked through the rest of the papers and photos.

"This must be Dr X. Perry-Ment," said Joe, holding up one of the prints.

"And this is a plan of part of his invention," Sam added. "I wonder what it does?"

More importantly, WHO was Dr X. Perry-Ment and why was the Smart Gang looking for him?

"It's up to us to find some answers," said Joe. "I'm sure that creepy duo are up to no good. There's something fishy going on."

But there was no time to sit and wonder what.

Polly heard voices growing louder. The Smarts were returning! Sam and Joe fumbled frantically with papers and photos, desperately trying to cram them back into the file. Polly began looking for a way out.

Joe ran to the secret door. But there was no lever to open it from this side.

Polly opened the door from the bakery, only to find the steps were rotten

Sam tugged frantically at the larder door but it was locked and wouldn't budge.

Polly thought of the scullery but there was nowhere to hide or escape to in there. Just in time, they dived for cover in the only place they could see to hide. Heavy footsteps stomped into the room.

Silently, Joe pulled out the guidebook and map. There MUST be another way out… and they had to find it, fast.

Can you find another way out of the kitchen?

In the Wine Cellar

While the duo searched the bakery, Joe heaved open the trapdoor. They jumped down onto the flight of stone steps below and Sam shut the door before the crooks returned.

They ran through a maze of dark passages until they reached the large wine cellar below the dining room. A strange green glow shone through what seemed to be a solid wall. It reminded Joe of the flashes they had seen the night before. The glow traced the outline of a door. Could it be another secret entrance and the way in to the Doctor's laboratory? Joe tapped the wall lightly.

Sam wondered if it was such a good idea to try to get in. But if the creepy Smart Gang were after the Doctor, surely they should be on his side. Meanwhile, Polly stared at what Sam was standing on and gazed around the cellar.

"An electrical circuit," she exclaimed, with a flash of inspiration. "Where's the note we found in the study? It tells us how to open the door."

Can you work out how to open the door?

125

Dr Perry-Ment Explains

There was a loud whirring sound and several clicks. The door slowly opened and they stepped through into a laboratory. At first, no one noticed the eccentric figure half hidden by a peculiar machine. But he had seen them.

"I know who you are," he said, looking alarmed. "You're working for the Smart Gang."

Polly tried to explain, but Dr Perry-Ment was still suspicious. If only they could prove they were nothing to do with the Gang. Suddenly Sam remembered. He did have something which belonged to the Doctor. If he gave it back, Perry-Ment would know they weren't working for the Smarts.

What has Sam got?

"Now I know you're on my side you can help me to spook the Smarts away," the Doctor said.

Joe, Polly and Sam looked a bit puzzled as the Doctor began to explain.

I am a scientist and I was working on a top-secret project when I made an amazing discovery…

… an incredible invention. But one of the junior scientists was working for the evil Smart Gang and they plotted to steal it.

I inherited the Manor 12 years ago, just as my granny had told me when I was a small boy.

The Manor seemed a perfect hiding place. I moved in and set up my laboratory here. My invention is a machine that moves people from place to place, instantly.

What could I do alone? A bodyguard will be here tomorrow, but in the meantime I decided to frighten the Gang by dressing up as a ghost. Now you're here it will be much easier.

I call it the IPT and it is working well. But so far, it will only move in Internal Mode.

Five days ago, I spotted figures outside; a face at the window. The Smart Gang had found me.

127

The IPT Machine

Polly and Joe looked doubtful. The Doctor's plan sounded crazy. But it was their only chance to outsmart the Smarts and help Perry-Ment. First, they would need some ghost outfits.

"The Gang are searching the house again. We'll surprise them in the Games Room," the Doctor said, hurrying off to the attic with Polly. "See you there."

Polly dug out an old white dress from the dressing-up box. She pulled it on and covered herself with smelly white powder.

Sam tried on the Doctor's ghost outfit. He had to make a few alterations to make it fit, but he thought he looked very spooky in the end. The first aid box gave Joe an idea. It took him ages to unwind all the bandages and wind them around himself, but he decided it would make a brilliant fancy dress.

At last they were ready. It was then that they realized they were trapped. The only door was the secret one they had come in by and neither could see how to open it from this side.

"I know," exclaimed Sam. "We'll use the machine."

But how did it work? Sam pulled the START lever. Instructions flashed onto the screen. He had seen the ZIP stick but what was the ZAP number? There weren't any numbers on the machine. Suddenly he gasped. In the screen he could see a face… the ghost! He watched in horror as it's arm reached out towards him.

But the ghost was trying to help them. It pointed at a book which was the IPT handbook. As they began to read, they realized they could work out the ZAP number and which keys to press on the machine.

What is the ZAP number? Which keys should they press?

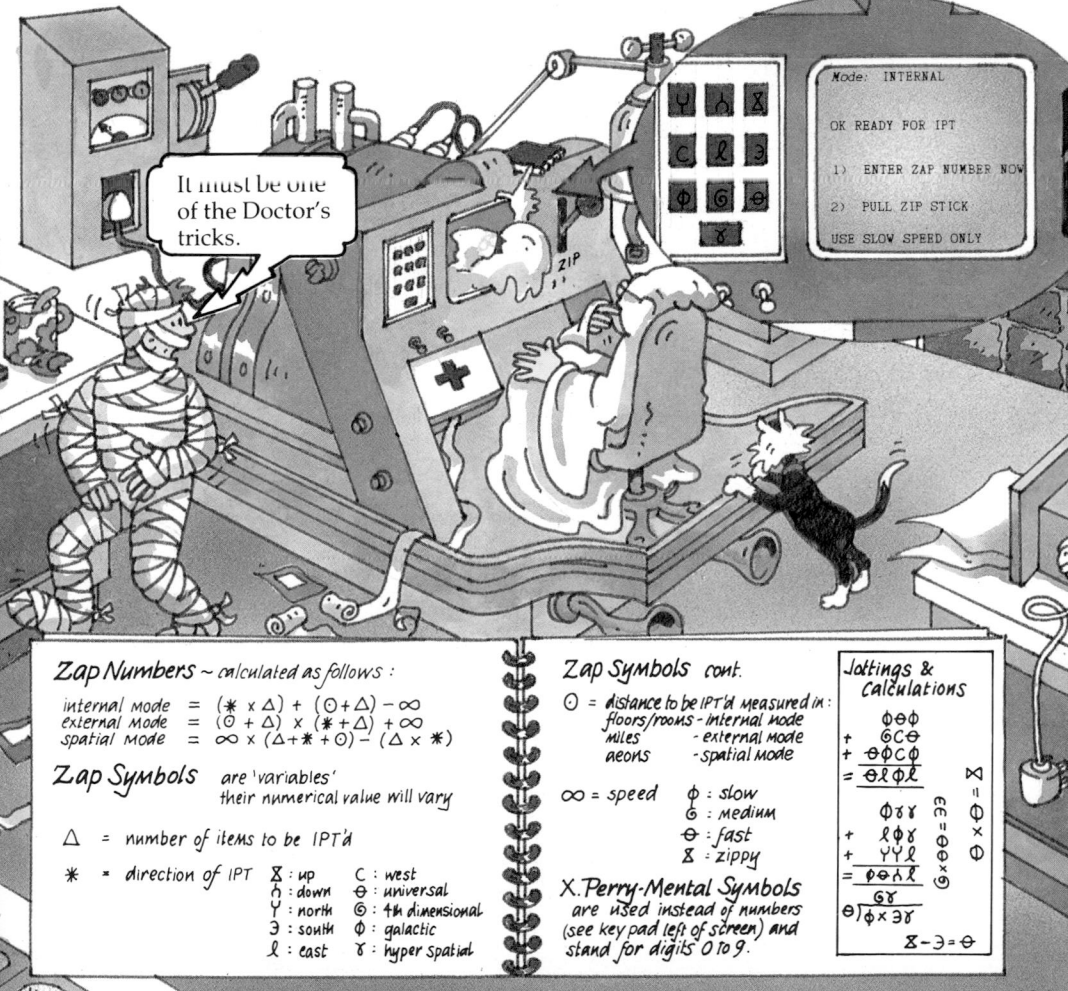

Ghostly Tricks

The machine whirred, buzzed and rattled. It finally shuddered to a stop in a cloud of green smoke. Sam blinked. With a start he realized they were in the library. Joe tapped in the ZAP number and sent the machine back to the laboratory.

Polly and Perry-Ment were hard at work in the games room. The Doctor was brushing florescent paint onto plastic skulls which made them glow eerily in the gloom and Polly was trying out a trick she had read about with dried peas, a glass and a metal tray.

Sam had an idea. He and Polly could be a headless ghost. He found her a black hood and then dashed behind a black curtain. As he balanced on a stool with his head tucked under Polly's arm, he tried to ask the Doctor about the ghostly figure.

My uncle used to put on magic shows here so there are lots of props.

The peas at the bottom swell and push out the ones on top. So they rattle down onto the tray and make a spooky noise.

But the Doctor was busy. He had decided to try an old trick from his uncle's book using a special chair and a mirror. His head was supposed to look as if it was floating in midair. But although he read and reread the instructions, he couldn't make it work. Finally he gave up.

Meanwhile, Polly and Sam had discovered a large mirror at the back of the stage with a lever to tilt it.

"Pepper's Ghost," exclaimed the Doctor. "That's one trick that will work."

He told Joe to jump into the pit and stand below the floodlight where he couldn't be seen. Sam was to carry on tilting the top of the mirror down towards the stage.

What will the audience see?

131

In Search of the Smart Gang

They ran to their ghostly positions as footsteps grew louder and closer. There were voices in the library, but they faded away as the steps carried on downstairs.

"There's someone in the hall," hissed Sam. "They're coming this way."

They came closer and closer… but no. They too carried on past.

"We'll just have to go after them," exclaimed Dr X. Perry-Ment.

Joe and the Doctor hurried into the library while Polly and Sam ran into the hall.

They tiptoed around the rest of the floor, peering cautiously into each room, but they found no one. Suddenly a board creaked behind them. Polly froze, then sighed with relief when she looked back. It was only the cat.

"Let's look downstairs," she said, feeling braver.

They crept down and stopped. Voices coming from the drawing room! This was scary.

What were they supposed to do now? Sam gulped and turned the handle slowly. There was silence on the other side of the door.

"Come on," Polly croaked.

They flung open the door and leapt into the room, trying to look as frightening as possible. BANG, CRASH, THUD. They collided with two other, very solid ghosts… Joe and the Doctor.

"This is useless," said Joe, picking himself up.

"We'll never scare the Gang like this," he added.

"Wait a minute," exclaimed Polly. "What's the time? I think I know where we can find all four Gang members together."

Where will they find the Gang?

Spooking the Smarts

The Doctor led the way to an incredible octagonal ballroom which was lined from floor to ceiling with mirrors. He held up his hand in front of one of the panels. It slid open and they stepped into a small, secret room, where they could hide and wait for the Gang. The walls were one-way windows and they could watch the ballroom. Although it was impossible to see into the room from outside.

All-Time Favourite Funeral Marches

The last to arrive was a sinister-looking girl wearing dark glasses. She seemed to be the boss.

"Well?" she snapped at the other three who looked very sheepish. "Have you found anything yet?"

Now was their chance. The Doctor released the panel. The four "ghosts" leapt out and the panel slid silently shut.

The Gang looked surprised, but not a bit frightened. Then suddenly the spy called Rex gasped. Seconds later, all four Gang members took to their heels. Looks of utter terror were on their faces.

Why? Joe and Polly were puzzled. Then Joe caught sight of something. Now he understood.

What frightened the Gang?

The Ghost in the Mirror

The ghost chased after the Gang, hovering in midair, howling. Joe, Polly, Sam and Perry-Ment raced after them. They reached the hall in time to see Rex cowering, petrified, by the front door.

He was desperately trying to open it. But at last he gave up and ran after the rest of the Smarts. With the ghost in hot pursuit, the Gang dashed along the corridor and straight on through the drawing room.

"Let me out of here!" yelled Rex, running into the dining room.

Joe and Polly watched from the door as the Smarts fumbled with one of the barred windows. The boss was already halfway through.

Seconds later, the last of the Gang clambered out. Polly, Sam and Joe ran into the room and watched incredulously as the ghost melted back into the mirror. Sam was sure the phantom smiled as it began to fade away.

"That's got rid of them," exclaimed Joe, watching the creepy quartet race away.

Sam stared at the mirror where the ghost had vanished. There was one final question.

Who was the ghost in the mirror? The Doctor smiled mysteriously. It was someone he knew very well. Polly thought she knew the answer.

Who is the ghost in the mirror?

Clues

Pages 102–103
Is there an open window? They can use the rope and hook.

Pages 104–105
Look for something to help them find their way around the house.

Pages 106–107
The window with the green light is on the first floor.

Pages 108–109
Think backwards.

Pages 110–111
Where do the footprints lead? Look at the book titles on page 108.

Pages 112–113
Try exchanging the last letter of the first word with the first letter of the second word.

Pages 114–115
This is easy. Use your eyes.

Pages 116–117
Use your eyes again.

Pages 118–119
Flick back through the book.

Pages 120–121
A different code is used on each document. Extra letters have been added to one.

Pages 122–123
Look at the map again. Where are they? Can you spot a hidden door?

Pages 124–125
Look at the note on page 109.

Pages 126–127
Has Sam picked anything up recently?

Pages 128–129
Hint:
Number of persons = 2
Direction = 9 (up)
Distance in floors = 2 (cellars to first floor)
Speed = 1 (slow)

Work out which X. Perry-Mental symbols stand for which numbers by solving the sums in the handbook.

Pages 130–131
Think hard and use your imagination.

Pages 132–133
Look at the mirror message on page 113. What is the time?

Pages 134–135
Look carefully at everyone in the ballroom and their reflections.

Pages 136–137
Look at the paintings and the family tree on page 107.

Answers

Pages 102–103

Using the pole with the hook, they pull down both ends of the rope pulley. The rope is hooked around the tyre and Joe sits in it, holding the pole. Polly and Sam hoist him up until he is level with the open window. He then hooks the pole on the window bar and swings himself inside. The tyre is lowered and Polly is hoisted up by Sam. Joe holds out the pole and drags her in. He then pulls in the free end of the rope using the pole. Polly and Joe lower the tyre again and then haul Sam up, again using the pole to drag him inside.

Tyre   Pole with hook   Rope pulley   Open window

Pages 104–105

Polly has spotted a guide and map to Grimstone Manor.

Pages 106–107

They should go to the study on the first floor which was where the strange glow came from on the previous night.

 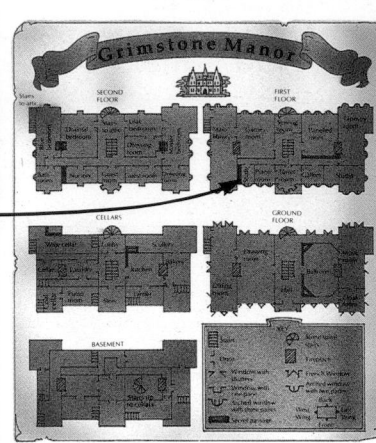

Pages 108–109

The note is written backwards. This is what it says with punctuation added:

To go from the dark to my secret cellar, look for the bottles and take out the Mellier. Press for the wine and press for the door, push right down or you will get no more. A glass on a bottle not a bottle by a glass. Place the jugs on the circle and then you will pass.

Remember

Pages 110–111

The footsteps go towards the bookcase which is the secret door. The handle is the book called HANDEL by I.M.A Lever.

Hidden lever 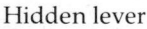   Footprints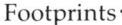

Pages 112–113

The message is decoded by swapping the last letter of each word with the first letter of the next. It says:

Search everywhere. The lab must be found. The machine will be mine. Meeting 15:30 hours, ballroom. The Boss. Code X

Pages 114–115

Joe is right. He has spotted the rear view of the ghost in the mirror, which clearly shows someone wearing a ghost costume.

Pages 116–117

The fireplace has changed which suggests it is a secret, revolving door and that there are two fireplaces.

The differences are ringed here.

Pages 118–119

They saw the girl standing outside Grimstone Manor on page 102.

Pages 120–121

The first document has one extra letter (or number) added in front of each group of letters. It is decoded by taking away the first dud letter and then amending the spacing to make words. It says:

THE SMART GANG DOSSIER 1

FACTS KNOWN

Name: Dr Xavier Perry-Ment

Born: 4 December 1950

Moved into Grimstone Manor in early September. Under Smart Gang surveillance since 10 September. World famous scientist working on top secret invention – Instant Physical Transference machine. Uses his own special code to work the machine in which symbols equal digits 0-9. Smarts still working to break code. He also sometimes uses a word code for his notes.

Code K

Pages 120-121 (continued)

The second document is decoded by swapping the first and last letters of each word. It says:

SMART GANG DOSSIER 2

Gang's uses for the machine:

could be rented to other crooks; entry to bank vaults, museums and galleries (and quick exits with loot leaving no trace); entry to government offices.

Operation Perry-Ment commences 12:00 hours on Saturday 24 September.

Code T

Pages 122–123

The map on page 106 shows a stone spiral staircase leading from the basement up to the cellars. This is in the room directly below the kitchen. You can see the hinges and edge of a trapdoor hidden below the rug where Polly, Joe and Sam are hiding.

Trapdoor

Pages 124–125

The door is opened by completing an electrical circuit. Polly works out how to do this from the coded note they found in the study on page 109.

They have to:

1) Remove the wine bottle labelled Mellier;
2) Press the wine press down;
3) Find the bottle with a glass on the label and take away the bottle and glass next to it;
4) Place the eight jugs on the dark stone slabs. (There are contact points on the slabs and also on the bottom of the jugs.) Sam is standing on the battery which powers the circuit.

Each item is ringed.

Contact points

Take these away

Wine press

Battery

Pages 126–127

Sam has Dr Perry-Ment's plan of the IPT motor. When the Smarts were returning on page 122, he crammed the yellow plan into his pocket without thinking. It is still in his pocket on page 125 in the wine cellar.

Page 122

The plan

Page 125

Pages 128–129

There are ten X. Perry-Mental Symbols and each one stands for a different number from 0-9. You can decode all the symbols by working out the Doctor's simple sums scribbled in the margin of the handbook.

X. Perry-Mental Symbols:

Ɣ	φ	⑥	⊖	c	ℓ	Ꝺ	Ⴤ	♭	X̄
0	1	2	3	4	5	6	7	8	9

The handbook shows the formulae for three Zap Numbers. The correct formula depends on the machine's Mode. The screen display shows the machine is operating in Internal Mode and says to use Slow Speed only.

The symbols used in the formula are explained in the list of Zap Symbols. The numbers they represent vary, but for Joe and Sam's move they are as follows:

Numerical value of each variable Zap Symbol:		X. Perry-Mental Symbols
number of people	= 2 (Joe and Sam)	⑥
direction	= 9 (up)	X̄
distance in floors	= 2 (cellar to first floor)	⑥
speed	= 1 (slow)	φ

So the equation to find the Zap Number is:

$$(9 \times 2) + (2 \times 2) - 1 = 21$$

The Zap Number is 21 and in X. Perry-Mental Symbols this is ⑥φ. These are the keys which Sam must press.

Pages 130–131

Pepper's Ghost is a famous trick. If Joe stands down in the pit so he can't be seen and the mirror is tilted, his image will be projected up onto the stage. The audience then see a ghostly image appear.

The diagram shows how Pepper's Ghost works.

Pages 132–133

They will find the Gang in the ballroom at 3:30 p.m. (15:30 hours).

The mirror message on page 113 is from The Boss, the leader of the Smart Gang and it arranges a meeting. Dr Perry-Ment's watch shows the time is now 3:20 p.m. They still have time to reach the ballroom before the Gang members arrive.

Pages 134–135

Polly, Joe, Sam and the Doctor are all reflected in the mirrors, but there is one extra ghostly figure who has no reflection. This must be a real ghost.

The real ghost.

Pages 136–137

The ghost is Mathilda, the Doctor's grandmother. Her portrait is in the family tree on page 107 and there is also a painting of her in the dining room. When you first see the portrait, Mathilda is frowning, but in the final picture her portrait is smiling after frightening away the Gang.

The ghost

Mathilda

The portraits . . . before and after

Before

After

First published in 1990 by Usborne Publishing Ltd, Usborne House, 83-85 Saffron Hill, London EC1N 8RT, England

The name Usborne and the device 🎈 are Trade Marks of Usborne Publishing Ltd.

Printed in Italy.